PRINTHOUSE BOOKS PRESENTS

I0643239

Overlords Karma

Miami's Urban Chronicles; Volume I

Thomas Barr Jr.

True Fiction

©Thomas Barr Jr.; 2014

PrintHouse Books, Atlanta, GA.

Published 4-25-2014

www.PrintHouseBooks.com

VIP INK Publishing Group; Incorporated

Cover art, designed by SK7.

ISBN: 978-0-9911719-5-8

Library of Congress Cataloging-in-Publication Data

   1. Urban Literature 2. Fiction 3.Political
     4. Thomas Barr Jr. 5.Miami, Florida

A policeman remembered the day of the death of Miami commissioner Amp Tate. Blood oozed over the marble floor of the most prominent news institution in Miami. Powerful commissioner Anthony "Amp" Tate laid stretched out with a gaping hole in his chest. With the gun still clutched in his hand, he attempted to speak to those gathered around him as he gasped his final breaths and died. Days before, Tate was indicted on corruption charges and profiled in Miami News as the City of Miami's most corrupt politician. Tate, a towering 6 foot -5 inch tall African American, was the commissioner of the only black district in Miami. He previously held the position as chair of the commission and was current head of the Overtown Development Corporation, with additional duties of entertainment permitting.

Tate a self-made man represented the interests and concerns of Miami's black community.

The policeman stationed in the lobby of the Miami News building rushed over when he heard the shot and screams. An elderly woman with her hands filled with a stack of papers fainted and littered the floor with her correspondences. The papers were soon matted with the commissioner's bright red blood as it leaked over the floor of the lobby. The cop stood over the commissioner uncertain what to do, as he had seen many fatal gunshot wounds of this sort. This man has bought it, he thought to himself. People scattered sprinting for the lobby stairway and exit doors. He yelled for someone to call 9-1-1. The cop jumped back from the body being careful not to get blood on his shiny black boots. Blood spewed from the hole in the commissioner's back as the bullet had ripped clean thru his chest. The cop looked on in pity as the commissioner's body initiated a series of involuntary jerks from his stiffened limbs. Two men initially in line ahead of the commissioner peered over the officer's shoulder at the body. "I wonder what he was trying to say," said one man looking down on the corpse.

■ ■

I dedicate this to Rose Marie and Thomas Senior, for their inspiration to aspire for greatness. I also dedicate this to Camillia Renee, Thomas Jacob, Jamal, Jazz, Gail and Latoya for their support and encouragement in writing this story. I additionally, dedicate this to my teachers whom encouraged me in my writing endeavors. Finally, I dedicate this book to all whom aspire to be more than what is defined by society and who positively touch the lives of others in this Journey we call life.

Thomas Barr Jr.

Overlords Karma

Miami's Urban Chronicles; Volume 1

VIP INK Publishing Group; Incorporated

Atlanta, GA.

Table of Contents

The Introduction

It was a sunny day, as Tate strolled into Overtown's community center in the heart of Miami. He scoped his surroundings looking for a nearby trash can to discard his empty juice container. He viewed a group of young men as they played basketball on the court. One tall lanky kid was about to go for a dunk and was flagrantly fouled by a shorter rotund kid with long arms. The shooter came down hard with a loud thud on the floor.

"Tough break kid," snorted Tate in his baritone voice as he headed to the front office.

He had an informal meeting with the department director and hoped to meet with him before the day got busy. The Overtown Community

Center was a state of the art building of modern design. The building contained high vaulted ceilings and glass walls throughout its design. The center's state of the art sports complex made it the city's Mecca for wayward youths.

As Tate rounded the corner he ran face to face into Terrence Kemp. Kemp was Head Director of Overtown's community center.

"How's it going Amp?"

He asked as he set his footing from the unexpected run in with the commissioner. Tate was a bit peeved with the unexpected bump in with the director. Tate disliked surprises and he especially disliked it when his toes got stepped on. Kemp a diminutive wiry framed man didn't possess an athletic bone in his body. It seemed odd that he would hold sway over athletic programs administered to city residents. Tate amused himself with that thought.

"Can't complain Terrence, I've been trying to reach you on your cell but was not able to catch up with you," said Tate his voice tinged with contempt. "I thought I would stop in and chat with you about the fundraising event I want to have in the district," he continued. "I could really benefit from you supporting me; I could use this facility as ground zero." As they stood in the hallway he eyed Terrence suspiciously for a response.

Terrence in a squeamish voice replied, "Let's step into my office for a bit Amp."

Terrence's office was full of exercise equipment and his desk was cluttered with case files.

"Amp my budget looks bleak this year, I'm not sure I could support that sort of event this year," said Terrence nervously clearing his throat.

Tate stood stoned face as he wrung his hands peering out the office window. He then turned, walked behind the desk and stood facing Terrence as their eyes locked.

"What does it take to get you on board with building this district to mirror Coral Gables or the Hamptons?" asked Tate.

Terrence paused for a minute and replied, "Effort."

***

Tate maneuvered his black SUV Cadillac through the congested traffic of the downtown Miami streets. He was happy and lighthearted as he drove thru traffic. He enjoyed driving a powerful SUV such as his. He sat up higher than the other cars and could feel the vibration of the engine titillate thru his fingers as he gripped the steering column. He mentally planned the specifics of the fundraiser and took care to be detailed in his timeline agenda. He successfully solicited the support of many district organizations to include Overtown's community center.

Tate considered himself a hands-on administrator. He enjoyed seeing projects develop and come to fruition. As he pondered, he pulled into the back alley of The Venetian, a residential and commercial condo complex. The Venetian was a towering art deco designed skyscraper. Many noted and well-connected Miamians utilized the facilities. He planned to meet with a couple of producers and artists concerning music projects they pitched him. He sat in his parked car, took out a long fat Cuban from his inside coat pocket. He lit it and blew the sweet aroma of its tobacco through his nostrils. The rush from the cigar made Tate feel elevated, as if he had hit a marijuana joint. Just as he took a second puff, there was a knock at his window. Tate let the window down and cut the engine on the Cadillac.

"How's it going Amp, you ready to hear some banging new tracks?" The young man said. "Yo... Sun, I been working for weeks on these joints!" He exclaimed in street lingo. Cigar smoke bellowed from the open window as Tate looked out, his eyes blood shot red from the smoke.

"The whole crew is in da studio, we're ready to show you some hot stuff." He eyed the skinny kid with dreads. Jeremy Coons was a neighborhood youth of Overtown and Tate had gone to college with his Aunt. Before Tate first won election he met the kid at one of his campaign rallies and was impressed by the kid's hustle. He seemed relentless in his pursuit to be a success in the music game.

Jeremy slipped him a CD, "Keep this for da ride and let's take the service elevator to the studio," he said. "But be careful when you play it Amp, the base will bump those speakers and expose that million dollar system of yours," Jeremy replied with a wide grin.

***

Tate stepped from the elevator and winced from the coldness of the room. I should've brought my coat he thought to himself. He entered a short corridor which led to a high ceiling room, with a glass enclosed booth in the center and leather couch chairs lining the walls. There was an office at the far end of the room; Jeremy motioned for Tate to enter. The group Haze and Mammoth were seated in the studio recording room, chatting about the performance they did last night. The group members of Haze were a multicultural mix of Latin, black and white youths. Members of the group called Mammoth were of Haitian descent which was reflected in their music. The studio walls were lined with large bass bin speakers. The electronics displays of the recording booth were highly technical. Jeremy hit a button on the large keyboard within the room and the thudding sound of 808 bass filled speakers vibrated with music.

***

Tate returned to his office in downtown Miami and contemplated his meeting with Jeremy's group. He felt anxious. He had always been a business man at heart and although he chose the public service route as a career, he considered himself an astute executive.   He believed like the blues, rap was a misunderstood music form. Its message is diverse as the many performers that promote the art. He could see the benefit in building a business model around the movement, which could benefit him personally as well as professionally.

Jeremy's groups have been getting positive feedback on a national level and they were a talented bunch of youth. He would resolve to keep Jeremy close so he would have inside knowledge on the group's progress. He had seen in many instances when non-business minded hustlers wasted money on street or youth founded art forms. One such example, street group DJ's, they yielded no return on investments for investors. The Group Honey Hill DJ's were very popular in the community and achieved regional acclaim back in the day. Tate believed if he had the opportunity of working with them in the community, he could have made them a national success with his professional business model. Ambition was a driving force for success and he had plenty of it. He had always been competitive in athletics as a youth and he loved the feel of empowerment in being good at a task. Such a feeling gave him a godlike confidence which he embedded in his persona.

His secretary buzzed him on the intercom to notify him of his pending luncheon at the Optimist Club. As he bounded out of city hall he ran into Raul Sancho, a politically conservative White American of Hispanic descent, "Amp are we still on for a round this weekend?" He responded with a quick nod and was out the door. He felt a pang of guilt in being curt with his response, but he needed to be on time for his appointment.

Sancho was one of the city commissioners along with Tate and he was a good ally when in session. He valued his relationship with Sancho. They often golfed and played an occasional hand of poker together. Sancho was a graduate of a local Ivy League school in the community, and was overall well respected. He was an aide to the former mayor and was said to have been groomed for the Miami political system. Sancho met Tate as an aide when Tate worked for a local nonprofit community center. They'd established a good rapport back in those days and worked on many community projects together. As they both rose in political positions respect became mutual between the two.

***

Tate whipped his Cadillac into valet parking outside the club; he pulled on his black suit jacket as he entered the establishment. He walked swiftly with wide strides and within a couple of seconds was thru the door. The Optimist Club was headquartered in a Mediterranean styled building with Terracotta roof tiles. Its many archways were flanked with leafy coconut trees. He was greeted by the mat idée, "Commissioner Tate your party is located on the outside patio." He gave a nod as he bristled pass the young man toward the back. He greeted the diners as he took a seat at the table. The luncheon had just begun moments ago and Tate was under the impression that he was horribly late. He was especially surprised to see Jeremy seated at the table, Jeremy shot him a quick salute. He felt a quick flash of apprehension as he looked away from Jeremy. His curiosity was peeked upon seeing him. The moderator of the luncheon, a balding gentleman with thick spectacles, discussed the local business owners concerns regarding the community. He listened intently with one burning question in the back of his mind, what the hell is Jeremy doing here?

***

Jeremy stood talking with individuals after the luncheon as Tate approached him, "How's it going?" Tate inquired.

Jeremy replied in the most professional voice he could conjure up, "Commissioner let me introduce you to a friend of mine Lisa Shilling."

Tate laughed inwardly thinking to himself what a house Negro. He then turned his attention to Lisa. Lisa Shilling was CEO of Light Star Entertainment, a nationally recognized music record label. She had young sparkling eyes and a pleasant smile. Her stature was tall and imposing as intimidating as her elegant beauty. Tate was not familiar with the company, but immediately thought of how he could better relations with Ms. Shilling.

"Lisa invited me to this luncheon and thought that it would be a good place for me to meet the community business owners," said Jeremy.

Tate said with a chuckle, "I was surprised to see you here Jeremy but you are definitely in good company," as he winked at Ms. Shilling.

She nodded and replied, "Commissioner."

"I hope to see you all at my upcoming fund raiser," Said Tate as he walked out to retrieve his car.

He had tested Lisa with his wink and she had taken it in stride. This meant she was a team player and well adept with dealing with powerful men. He would need to watch her.

Many of Tate's associates viewed him as a man of appetite; however he viewed himself as a regular guy with a working class upbringing. His parents were from the south; his grandfather had been a sharecropper. His grandmother was the local beautician for black women in their small town in Georgia.

Tate was programmed from an early age to be the best at whatever he endeavored. Success was the American dream which translated into money, respect, and power. He saw glimpses of this growing up as a kid in Georgia. As he would go out with his grandfather to the tobacco fields to work men respected him. His grandfather was a hard worker and a man's man when associating with people. His personality was gruff, direct and to the point. He had endured long years of share cropping and dishonest bank loan agents. This in turn gave him little patience for entertaining foolishness.

***

Tate tried to emulate this character in his dealings with people as he navigated thru life. He phoned his secretary after leaving the luncheon to inquire about his fund raiser. He planned to have it in the district, accessible to the community. However his wife insisted that it be at the home in order to exude a more family values appeal.

***

Cherry Tate was a college professor and held a PhD from a prestigious Ivy League school from the Northeast part of the nation. She met her husband while in graduate school, got married and conceived

Tate Junior. Cherry was an attractive, tall women that dressed and looked the part of a trophy wife. Cherry's family was from the New England states and they prized education. Self-reliance was always taught in her household as a child by her parents, who both were educators.

He phoned Cherry as he sat in his car in the parking lot of the restaurant. "Hey honey how is your day going?" He asked.

"Excellent," chirped Cherry. "Have you given much thought to your fund raising party?" Cherry inquired.

He felt uneasy letting strangers into his home and was suspicious of spies. He believed in not giving his enemies ammunition. He knew Cherry wanted to show off her home and interior decorating skills publicly; which could jump start her entrepreneurial ambitions. He preferred a more public venue for the event, but feared he would have to relent to the wishes of his wife.

"I'm still working out the details in my head, but you will certainly be the first to know," replied Tate.

He instantly thought he may need help in organizing the intricate details of his fund raising event. He was vaguely familiar with one of his constituents, whom wrote him concerning completing volunteer time with his office. As he concluded his call with Cherry, he gave his office a call.

"I need the number for any constituents that offered volunteer services in my district," said Tate.

"Just a minute sir," replied the secretary, "The name is Ray Sutter."

"Great," replied Tate, "Text me the contact info."

He pulled out of the parking lot and turned his car towards the interstate. He considered taking the quick route to his district and traffic was light today.

As he drove he clicked on the radio and the DJ had just announced the next song playlist. The DJ caught Tate's attention as he mentioned the last group.

"We got a banging new song from the group Haze, they are home grown," replied the DJ.

***

Tate pulled up to 411 East State Street located in the more seedy part of the neighborhood in Overtown. It was a white dainty house with a wraparound porch that sat behind a white picket fence. Tate swung the front gate open walked up the steps and rang the doorbell twice. A tall older woman with silvery gray hair, styled in a long pony tail, answered the door.

"Can I help you?" She quipped.

"Yes I'm looking for Ray Sutter," Tate replied.

"That's my son," the woman said. "Come on in commissioner and have a seat, I'll get Ray for you," the women said in a wry voice.

The women led Tate to the Florida room; which consisted of a worn T.V., tattered sofa and a few bamboo chairs with the seat backs missing.

"I'm surprised you knew who I was," Tate replied.

"Everyone in this community knows of you," remarked the women as she gestured for him to be seated and exited the room.

In a dark smoked filled room lay a slight figure of a man lounging on a small twin sized bed. A small black and white television played in the background with the volume turned down low. The door of the room opened.

"Lord Ray you act like your still in the pen," said the women with the pony tail.

The ash end of the cigar lit up as Ray Sutter took a long pull of his stogie.

"That's how I feel living with you," he replied to his mom.

She chuckled, "Clean ya self-up you got a visitor."

Ray Sutter a black Latino was a natural born U.S. citizen, his mom was from Cuba and his dad was from South Bronx, New York. He had a slight build, black wavy hair and was an ex-felon. He had contacted Tat's office weeks ago to do some volunteer hours for his probation requirement. In prison he took up boxing and was rather quick with his hands. He fought on the prison circuit and had a record of undefeated with a 100% knock out rate in the ring. He spoke fluent Spanish so white Latinos would often take their foot out their mouths when making disparaging remarks of him, not knowing he understood them.

"Ray," Tate replied as the ex-felon entered the room.

"How are you commissioner, I am honored to have you in my home," Ray shot back.

As Tate stood the two shook hands, Tate was a good three feet taller than Ray. Tate sized him up physically, but would see what raw moral substance the ex-con was made of.

"I hear you want to do some volunteer work for me," asked Tate.

"Yes I do but I have to let you know up front that I am an ex-con," stated Ray sternly.

Tate liked playing it straight but often found he had to play dirty when the need called for it. In politics it was hard to play fair when everyone else was playing dirty. He represented the only majority black district in the city and had to play hard ball with other politicians in getting things done. Ray would be perfect in building a coalition in getting things done for his fund raisers in the Latino community. He could also be useful down the line if he was successful with this job Tate thought to himself.

"No problem your honesty says it all," Tate replied shaking Ray's hand a second time.

31

***

Tate seemed content in his spirit about how things for his planned fund raiser were turning out. He planned to hold the event at Kemp's place in the district, but because Cherry insisted that it be at their place, he would have to go along with her plans. His inner thoughts would not let Terrance Kemp off so easy. He would utilize the community center for his fundraiser in another way. He decided to assign him the task of setting up a Tel-la-thon for fundraising activities in the district. Such an event would be good publicity for circulating his name in the community and it could serve essentially as headquarters for the reelection committee. A black commissioner often does not have the support of the mainstream business firms and developers in bankrolling campaign fund raising efforts. The grass roots effort is a more viable and acceptable avenue of operation in the Overtown district. Tate believed that Terrence Kemp could mobilize the grass root effort, making the community center the central hub of operations.

Terrence Kemp and Tate had a good professional working relationship in the Overtown community. Within the professional arena blacks were held to a different standard of operation as compared with other professionals. Their operations were more closely scrutinized, as he often would reminded Kemp on functional processes of the community center. Tate frequently remembered growing up as a kid his father telling him that he should work ten times as hard as the average white man on a job. He never truly understood this until he started work in the real world. While he would be on a job with other workers in a diverse setting he was not safe to feel secure as the others. For the works of black employees were more readily scrutinized than all others.

He made calls to schedule an appointment with his barber at Beale Street. Beale Street was a local community barber in the Overtown district. Most of the black professional bourgeoisie came through for light networking; as well as cosmetic touch ups, haircuts, etc. Tate also made arrangements for Terrence Kemp to meet him at Beale Street.

■■

It was bright and sunny outside of Beale Street Barbershop and the air held a sea salt ocean beach smell. The barbershop was located in Tate's Overtown district. It was a stucco designed store front located among the many retail shops of Beale Street. Tate walked into the shop and was instantly greeted by a dreadlock haired brown complexioned man.

Speaking with a heavy Jamaican accent the man said, "Hello commissioner Tate, have a seat rite here mon."

The barber was Movay Garvey; he's a well-known community barber who cuts hair for NFL, NBA and other professional athletes. He was well connected in this way, when black athletes want a recharge of the black cultural experience they often look up Movay. They're guaranteed to not be harassed and just hang out with genuine fellas for a minute or two.

"Same cut," Tate replied as he sat in the barber's seat.

Movay replied, "Terrance should be in directly."

The shop was a bustle with music blaring and multiple conversations going on at one time. Tate shut his eyes to relax while being lined up by Movay. He could hear one guy talking about his baby's momma and how she was threatening him with child support if he pissed her off in any way. Another guy talked about the best all-time NBA player and how much money he made. One other guy was talking about who was the biggest street hustler back in the day and how he met his demise. The shop walls held autographed commemorative photos of celebrity patrons; such as Rick Ross and Dewayne Wade among others.

Terrence entered the shop and took a chair beside Tate, "Line me up," he said to the barber.

"Amp," he said. "I talked with Chris Mogoya and he is interested in developing a site located on the community center property." Terrence commented. "He is interested in building a housing condo complex with merchant shops in the lobby," he said. "This could boost the profile of the center and generate revenue for the district."

"I plan to work with him on some of the details and we will be meeting later in the week," said Terrence.

Changing the conversation, "I heard you were going to have the fund raiser at the house so here is a grass roots donation to help out."

Terrence leaned over and slipped a check into Tate's pocket. Tate had not said a word, but continued to keep his eyes shut as he took in the surrounding bustle of the shop. Terrence all lined up, stood shook the hair from his coat and slipped out the shop.

Tate was not sure what to make of Terrence's revelation about having one of the community center's site developed. He had heard of Chris Mogoya, but had never met him. Chris was known as a carpet bagger, he moved from city to city exploiting communities for financial gain in the opinion of most. Terrence was young and in Tate's opinion a little naïve.

"All done commissioner," said Movay as he applied rubbing alcohol around the shape up.

"I will apply it to your tab," said Movay as Tate walked out the shop.

■■

Tate entered his office in downtown Miami and as he passed the receptionist she handed him a brown envelope.

Tate replied, "Thanks," and continued on to his inner office. As he walked in the doorway he was greeted by his secretary.

"Good Afternoon commissioner," she said. "Would you like coffee sir?"

He replied, "No thanks," closing his door, he sat behind his desk.

He plopped the brown envelop down and opened it. It was a note from Commissioner Raul Sancho, *Tate I've scheduled a meeting with some people and I want you to join me*, the note read. There was an address and directions listed. The meeting was to be a brunch scheduled tomorrow morning at the golf pro shop. He rocked back in his chair and thought what in the world could this be about. He then made a few calls and headed home for the day. "Forward all my messages to my cell," he said to the secretary as he walked out.

■■

Sitting in his study Tate pulled the check from his pocket; *thirty thousand dollars certified* it read.

"That's my boy," Tate said aloud as he placed the check into his home safe under his desk. Tate was overcome with a sudden impulse to read.

He pulled an old tattered law journal from his library shelf and thumbed through it. He had completed a couple of law courses while in graduate school. He loved reading legal briefs and old case law. There was a page that was folded with a page tag attached. He opened the folded page and read the highlighted subtitle, *Beyond the Scope of Law.* He continued to read. Death precludes prosecution of a proposed defendant in any court of law.

He heard the doors to his study push open and Tate Jr. entered.

"How's it hanging dad," he yelled.

"A little to the left son, a little to the left," Tate chuckled as he greeted his son.

Tate Jr. was 7 years old, the only child of Tate and Cherry. Tate Jr. was a big kid for his age and Tate worked with him on his sports endeavors every chance he got. Tate wanted the best for his son and supported him in all his endeavors. He tried to make every little league game and parent teacher conference. He was also careful not to let his career aspirations diminish his family life. Legacy was very important to Tate's father which was instilled in Tate as he became a man. The key to prosperous black families is a successfully taught son he thought to himself.

"Junior did you practice your passing technique today," he said to Tate Jr.

"Yes sir," Tate Junior replied. "I worked out for an hour dad!" He exclaimed.

"Good job you need to do that also with you studies," said Tate. Tate was heavy into athletics as a youth and as he matured he realized the importance of academics in college. He wanted to teach his son how to balance the two.

Tate Junior replied as he kicked an imaginary rock, "You always say that dad, I know."

Cherry stuck her head in the door, "You guys ready for dinner, I made Chili," she said with excitement in her voice.

"Let's eat," said Tate to his family.

Tate returned to his study after dinner to look over a few things scheduled on his out of office work itinerary. He had a few meetings scheduled for the entire week and a morning brunch with Raul the next day. He made a mental note to himself to meet up with Jeremy as soon as possible to see what was going on with the music thing. He heard the release on the radio from Haze earlier and it sounded pretty good. He also was thinking he should have them perform at his event to give them some exposure and for networking purposes.

He thought to himself he would have Cherry call his secretary for a contact sheet in the morning and have his invitation sent out as soon as possible. He thought about Ray also and how he would fit in to his planning for the fund raiser. He would need to schedule another meet with Ray to lay down the law and let him know what time it was. He was unsure rather to keep Ray off the books as a type of body guard or keep him on as a personal assistant. After all Ray was an ex-con and could bring negative attention to him when he less needed it. However, he could be seen as representing rehabilitation efforts in revitalizing the community.

"People first, generate economics second!" He exclaimed. "I've just developed my campaign slogan," said Tate aloud.

■■■

Miami Gardens Golf was a well-manicured clubhouse that catered to South Florida's finest residents. With its wooden doors, courtyard patios and arcades the architecture was impressive. It was a well-entrenched establishment that has been around since the late 40's and 50's in the community. A lot of old money hung around the place many west palm beach golf pros played casual rounds for club promotional purposes. Tate strolled into the lobby around 10am and was met by Raul's staff person. He led Tate down a side hallway onto a closed in patio which served as a cigar room.

"Good morning Amp," Raul said as he sat puffing on a cigar.

The assistant shut the door and the two sat alone in the room as CNN blared on a 62" flat screen over a bar.

"Have a cigar?" Raul said.

"Not before lunch," replied Tate.

He figured Raul sought to give him the rundown of what was to happen before the meeting. Raul represented the Latin syndicate and what he says goes.

"Amp I'm going to be straight with you," Raul said. "I am working with a developer on a couple of projects. One of those projects for example is to bring casinos to downtown Miami and I want your support." He said. "I need the support of the African American community and that's you." Raul stated. "We take care of each other on the commission and I have always seen that you were taken well care of," said Raul.

Tate thought to himself that he had to play this situation smart as a black commissioner. He despised him for his manipulative ways but had to respect him. If he went against Raul he could face alienation in commission votes regarding important issues pertaining to his district. He was also a minority on the commission and depended heavily on coalition building to close on any proposed new projects pertaining to his constituency. Tate was being forced to make a commitment, he decided to play it safe and cover himself. It was not a matter of trust but one of self-preservation.

Tate stated, "I am with you 100% Raul but I will not be able to stay to meet with your guys for the meeting." Tate folded his arms. "I am working with a donor and need to be at a workshop regarding fundraising for my campaign."

Raul puffed an O ring of smoke as Tate talked.

"I do think that downtown casinos could generate a lot of revenue," said Tate.

He knew he would have to convince Raul that he would not rock the boat on this. Raul lowered his cigar and looked Tate squarely in the eye.

"Amp do not jerk me around on this issue," said Raul, "There is a lot of money to be made on this thing," he straightened his tie. "I suppose checking on your own dollars is a good enough reason to sit this one out," chuckled Raul as he slapped Tate on the back. Tate almost choked as he coughed.

"I will be in touch," said Tate as he exited the room.

"Sure you will," Raul replied as he walked Tate to the door.

Tate could foresee a major issue with this whole developer slash casino dilemma and knew he had only bought time to devise his own strategy for dealing with it. He would not want to shake hands with anyone on a deal before deciding his true feelings of an issue. He dodged meeting with Raul's developer friends because of this exact reason. Tate knew that he was measured at a different standard than Raul in the eyes of the public. Tate was a black politician and walking that fine line of fat cats versus community need was an art form.

The phone rang. In a darkened, smoke filled room the T.V. is on tuned down to a faint lull. A flickering shadow of a person lay slumped off a twin sized bed, fidgeting in ashtrays strewn around the floor underneath the bed. There was a knock at the door.

"Ray," the person said from the other side. "Pick up you got a call from the commissioner."

Ray picked up the phone in his room.

"Hang up," he yelled out. "Yes Sir," Ray replied into the mouth piece of the phone.

He listened intently.

"Got it," Ray again replied. "Will do," said Ray as he put down the receiver.

He lit a cigarette butt and took a long drag. There is another knock at the door and a voice asked, "What he wants?"

Ray replied, "Mom will you mind your business and get me a new suit!" He smiled inwardly. "I need a black suit," he said under his breath to himself.

Fund Raiser

Tate's residence was located on the Intracoastal Waterway, which was near the entry point to the main part of the city. It was of contemporary architectural design with hints of tropical attributes. He stood on his bedroom balcony inhaled the South Florida air and absorbed the sun rays of the cloud less sky. Off in the distance he could see a couple of Kayakers and Pontoon boats as they made their way in the tranquil waters. He was not much of an outdoorsman, however, he remembered going fishing with his father and playing in the water scaring the fish away. Need-less to say his father stopped taking him fishing. He smiled to himself of those fond memories of his childhood growing up as a rambunctious kid.

Cherry entered the bedroom.

"Babe we have all the details in order for the fundraiser tonight and you're going to love it," she chirped.

She waited with anticipation for his response. She knew he had been hesitate about her pitching in with his planning details.

"I have an Afro Latin Jazz Orchestra coming in from New York, great food, a chocolate fountain and drinks."

Tate answered back, "great honey."

He tried to maintain an expressionless demeanor.

She grabbed her keys.

"I'm off see you later tonight," she said as she walked out the room.

The keys jingled as she walked, the sound faded as she departed the residence. Tate let out an exhaustive sigh. He had been orchestrating tonight's event for months and felt mentally spent. He knew he had to really turn it up a notch for a good show at the gala later. He thought to himself the meeting with Jeremy would be a good boost for his morale. The thought of making money was always a vigorous stimulator Tate smiled to himself.

***

Tate confirmed his order to pick up his Tux; he threw on his street gear and headed out to meet up with Jeremy. Jeremy stood on the corner outside the studio and scrolled through text messages on his cell phone. He had gotten a text from Tate and was waiting for him to pull up any minute. Jeremy had been doing a lot of foot work to make his group successful and had established many good contacts. Tate tapped Jeremy on his shoulder as he looked through his phone. He spun around with his fists up in a guard up stance.

"What's up Dude," He looked frazzled. "You scared me," exclaimed Jeremy!

Tate chuckled and replied "let's see what you got cooking in the studio."

They walked into the studio and the group Haze was inside the booth room performing. A few members of the group Mammoth was sitting around the engineering board observing the producer fine tweak the melodic music booming from the speakers. Tate heard Haze's latest single on the car radio a while back and was surprised their songs were on the radio so quick.

Tate inquired, "How did you guys get radio play so quick?"

Jeremy replied with a smile "Lisa."

Tate thought to himself Lisa seems to think there is something to this group or she would not be doling out cash like that.

Tate said, "Listen Jeremy with things starting to pick up you guys need representation."

Jeremy replied, "You took the words right out of my mouth."

He pointed at Tate.

"I wanted you to be our manager but I didn't know how you would take it, you being in politics and all," said Jeremy.

Tate replied, "I'm your man; hip hop is a business just like any other." He rubbed his palms together. "I have some great ideas to get us on the national scene," he exclaimed.

"Yeah I'm with that but, one question, how do we get the best record deal," Jeremy asked.

Tate being a musician in his youth had working knowledge of the artist signing process in the music business. He played the trumpet and his teacher was a Jazz player who was signed to a major deal in the late 70's.

Tate said, "Let's have lunch and we can discuss this at length."

***

Ruby's was a well-known lunch spot for the professional working class. It was a jalopy of a place which represented a throwback to the old juke joints of the south. They specialized in chicken wings and beer. Tate entered with Jeremy and was seated by the waitress in a booth with a view by pool side.

"Listen Jeremy" Tate said, "First we need to generate our own buzz in getting the music out to the public."

Tate tapped his index finger on the table.

"Being on the radio is a good first start but we need to do more."

Jeremy replied, "Cool but I need some food." Jeremy rubbed his stomach in a circular motion.

He being a slender fellow, Tate imagined he had little use of food as his weight was a buck O five.

Tate motioned to a waitress.

"Give us a bucket of wings, fries and pitcher of beer," he said.

The waitress scribbled something on a note pad and wiped the table with a damp cloth before disappearing behind the counter.

Tate turned to Jeremy, "Listen here's how it's going to work."

He lowered his voice. "If you want to prove to a record label you are worth getting signed, you first need to show them you can make it without them."

Tate twisted in his seat. "In other words, you have to do all the promotional work, getting shows, and more all by yourself." Jeremy nodded his head in agreement. "If you then reach a level where you have a good amount of fans behind you and you can prove that these fans make you money, you have a much better chance of getting offered a record deal." He leaned closer to Jeremy. "In fact, record labels will start approaching you as they will want a piece of the action."

Jeremy replied, "So basically we need a fan base or a following."

"Jackpot," shouted Tate. The waitress prepared the table placing wings, fries and beer in the center with utensils on the side.

Jeremy grabbed a wing and said, "We can definitely do business with Lisa."

Tate replied, "That's if she gives us the best deal."

Jeremy responded, "I think that she has our best interest at heart."

Tate eyed Jeremy suspiciously, "And why is that he asked?"

"I just know she does and let's leave it at that." Jeremy replied.

Tate stood, "I have to get going I have a ton of things to do before it gets too late." He looked at his watch. "I will draw up the papers stipulating myself representing you as management."

Jeremy stuck out his hand. "No need for that you know we go way back, you my man," he said.

Tate shook Jeremy's hand and was out the door. He had second thoughts about affirming the deal unofficially but against his better judgment he pushed it to the back of his mind. Besides he was the consummate mover and shaker. He now had something to officially build on, without the limitations of public regulation and bureaucratic red tape.

***

Tate was excited about the development of the music deal and sensed good vibes from the meeting with Jeremy. The fund raiser was paramount so Tate decided to make a few calls to check the progress of its planning. Years ago when Tate won his first election he was advised by his mentor to form a Political Action Committee to help with his campaign. He raised over two million dollars in his first election run. He paid off his campaign debt and donated the rest to a local college educational charity. They named a college dormitory after him. This time as head of his own PAC he would use the money for his personal use upon losing office or retirement. Tate drove to his office and was greeted at the door by his secretary.

"Commissioner I emailed the contact list to your wife concerning the fund raising event," she said.

She waited pensively for Tate's response as she knew anything related to fundraising could have an adverse effect in regards to his mood. She had grown to know Tate's personality due to years of service in his office.

"Thanks," said Tate as he strode into his office. He flopped down behind his desk and began making calls.

***

Party Formal by Shay was a business located in Tate's district that rented and sold formal attire. It was Korean owned and was the only store in Tate's district of its kind. Many black entrepreneurs overlooked the money making opportunity of such a venture. Many of them were afraid to operate out of the paradigm of the proverbial box. The phone rang the front desk salesperson picked up, "Shay's formal," In a thick Asian accent she chirped into the receiver. "Yes commissioner everything is ready for pick up." The machines in the shop buzzed loudly. "Your wife will be in later for the package," said the salesperson. "Oh you're parked out front," The salesperson exclaimed in surprise. "Ok great I will bring your things out to you." The salesperson hung up the phone and grabbed a package on the way out the door. Tate's car was in front of the store backed in, he popped the trunk.

The sales person placed the packaged in the trunk and Tate replied, "Put it on my tab." "Yes sir," she responded.

Tate drove off as he continued to focus on his mental checklist in preparation for the fundraiser.

Cherry in the meantime had made contact with the manager for the band, organized the caterers and coordinated the decorations for the house. As Tate pulled in the drive way the house was full of people getting things prepared for the fundraiser. Tate entered the house amongst the bustle of caterers and began preparation for his evening of swooshing invited fat cats out of their money. Cherry's event planning called for a number of raffles for various artworks and art deco sculptures culminating in a final auction. As Tate dressed he began going through his mental checklist of possible top donors that would be attending the party. He was very keen about remembering the little incidental facts of a person regarding family, friends, etc. He felt he was mentally in spirit for the fundraiser and his role as artful facilitator.

***

The clanging of expensive Schott Zwiesel goblets could be heard as guests mingled in the lobby of Tate's home. NFL owners, NBA players, actors and community leaders were among the guest parlaying before dinner. Tate shook hands with anyone he encountered and told jokes as he maneuvered through the crowd. The band played an old jazz calypso and a few guests began to dance the waltz as people continued to enter the venue. Tate saw Jeremy enter with Lisa Shilling and headed over to greet them.

"Boss man," Jeremy replied as he slipped a check into Tate's outstretched hand, before shaking it.

"Hello Lisa," Tate said as he slipped the check into his pocket with a broad smile. Tate leaned into

Jeremy and asked, "Where the hack did this come from?"

Jeremy replied, "This is a fundraiser lets fundraise" as he led Lisa in direction of the band.

Tate was approached by a short guy with horned rimmed glasses, "Nice home commissioner," the guy said. "I have an interest in buying exotic homes," he went on, "and I believe you have a great taste in your selection." Tate sensed that the gentleman was trying to befriend him so he decided to entertain the chap.

"I love the space myself," replied Tate. "Like I heard from a good source there is no place like home," Tate said with a chuckle.

The man adjusted his spectacles and went on to say "commissioner I like the fire and initiative you bring to your office and hate to see a decent person such as yourself sully your humanity in the hustle of South Florida politics." He cleared his throat. "I am a writer by trade and I would like to chat more with you about building your brand." Tate thought to himself a writer could be very useful in his campaign.

Cherry came up and took Tate by the elbow; he shot a quick "excuse me" to the gentlemen. Cherry led Tate to the corridor and gave him a big kiss.

"Ok babe you're up," she said. "We're beginning the raffle and it would be great if you could mingle to promote it," she said.

He straightened his tie and replied, "Let's get it on then."

He believed that his district faced the problems of flawed economics, cultural degradation and city politics in addressing social concerns. He believed the problems that faced his district could not be solved by him or social activists. The system was the problem which needed to be changed for a more comprehensive redress of social problems. Tate addressed the audience, "As I officially announce my intentions to run for re-election to district five. I support the belief that the cries of poor and disenfranchised people are not simply caused by men alone, nor will they be solved by men alone. However, I am the man who will affect the much needed change process if you support my candidacy." The audience erupted in cheers and applause as the band began playing the old musical tune anchors away.

He was pulled to the side by an usher, "Sir you have a visitor in the front gardens," said the young lady. Tate nodded and made his way through the crowd towards the direction of the gardens. The crowd bustled and people clamored about readying for the raffle that was about to begin. Tate spotted Jeremy and Lisa in what seemed an intense discussion off from a main crowd of people. Tate thought to himself I wonder what that topic was all about as he walked on through the crowd.

Tate entered the garden area and instantly smelled the heavy sweet scent of cherry tobacco that lingered in the air. A figure stood with his back facing Tate with a Kangol hat on as smoke bellowed profusely from his lit cigar.

"That's you Ray?" asked Tate.

Ray replied, "Nice home commissioner." He took a drag. "Looks like you had a successful showing."

"I hope it reflects more in the green showing if you know what I mean," chuckled Tate. Ray tapped his cigar and watched the ashes fall to the ground in light orange ambers.

"I decided to check in with you to find out when you want me to start," said Ray.

"Well my intentions were for you to work with me until after the election," replied Tate. "I planned to call you in to the office in the morning to introduce you to a couple of folks," said Tate. "Can you be in at 10:30?" "We can do lunch afterwards," Tate offered.

"That's great," Ray replied.

"In the meantime stay and enjoy the festivities," said Tate.

"Thanks but I promised my mom I would bring her dinner." Ray put out his cigarette and stuck the butt into his pocket. "I will see you in the morning," he replied.

Tate thought back to the letter that he received from Ray and how an impression he made upon him when he read it. Ray an ex-con had served his debt to society and was trying to turn his life around. Tate thought a fight against the recidivism rate in the community would be a good platform to run on in his election. Ray's letter touched on the fact that he grew up in a violent household which led to his future problems with the law. He did stints in juvie as a kid and served time for aggravated battery netting him a couple of years in prison. A prison sociologist believed his behavior bordered on sociopathic behavior. Ray himself stated in his letter that he believed it was a choice to exercise such a behavior and not an illness.

Tate believed Ray could be helped and with community support in acquiring meaningful work, could be rehabilitated. Tate felt that his intent was to help Ray in any way possible to get him acclimated to society. Tate watched Ray as he exited the garden headed towards the street to retrieve his car. "See ya Ray," he said as he rejoined the festivities.

Tate knew in order to raise substantial amounts of money for his campaign he needed to appease key players in corporate Miami. Tate knew he himself straddled the fence on pro-business affairs and considered the needs of the community above all else. In building a fundraising machine Tate knew a solid base was needed. Hedge-fund managers throughout the city regularly have dinners and social events. Many politicians attend these functions and network with various business entities. Tate knew that Raul Sancho was one of the major organizers of these events and eventually he would have to deal with Raul in his own way.

Tate walked in while the auction was taking place and immediately made eye contact with Raul Sancho. Raul tipped a wine glass in Tate's direction and he nodded back in Raul's direction. Ten thousand to the lady in back the auctioneer blared over the microphone as the auction ended with an applause. Cherry ran up to Tate with excited gestures, "Babe you were auctioned for ten thousand dollars," she said in excitement.

Tate replied, "Fabulous this fund raiser has been a great success." He kissed his wife. "This is just the beginning baby," he said to Cherry. "We're definitely off to a great start."

Tate wondered who had won the auction and what it entailed on his part he was anxious to meet this obligation. He initially thought having an auction as a fundraiser was silly and he preferred more serious endeavors. He probably would have to donate time for a business luncheon or do a photo opt he thought as he pondered the issue.

Lisa and Jeremy toasted as the auction ended in applause, they were ecstatic that the auction was a success. Lisa's secretary approached her and inquired, "Ms. Shilling what am I to do with this auction ticket?"

Lisa said, "Why my dear you must cash that in, you've just received a ten thousand dollar bonus in your salary for the month."

***

Raul and The Empowerment Trust

Tate served as commission chair and head of the Overtown Development Corporation, which oversaw economic development initiatives in the community. He often felt he was voted into leadership by the commission as a shield to cover for any illicit activities of other members. Raul walked into Tate's office as Tate was hanging up the phone.

"How's it going Amp? Got a minute?" Raul asked.

What can I do you for commissioner," Tate replied as he reared back in his office chair.

Raul replied, "I want to fill you in on the meeting you were unable to attend at the club house. Chris Mogoya is a developer out of New Orleans,

Louisiana and he is submitting a proposal to develop parts of Miami."

"Mogoya," replied Tate, "yes I have heard of him." Tate with a wrinkled brow continued. "He has proposed to construct a pharmaceutical park and high tech modern casinos in the downtown district and would like the Overtown Development Corp to take a look at his proposal."

Raul walked over to a window in Tate's office and peered out.

"There is no need to take bids on this sort of thing Amp, I believe Mogoya Enterprises Inc. to be the best in the industry," said Raul.

He straightened his tie and paced the tiled floor of Tate's office.

Tate made doodles on a nearby note pad on his desk as Raul discussed his already made decisions for the project. Tate wanted to be respected by his peers and be viewed in high esteem as any office holding representative of the people. His conscious was not always in equilibrium with the running's of the inside politics of the process. Tate knew little of this Mogoya fellow, yet Raul was backing the guy with no hesitation. Tate knew Raul had links with many subcontractors which could make him a powerful person within his district and throughout South Florida.

"In addition my office will handle all required documentation and communication related to the project," said Raul. His hands stuffed in his pockets, he rocked back on his heels as he spoke.

Tate shifted in his chair and replied, "I would feel much better about this if we could assign a subcommittee to serve as an intermediary."

"Fine my office will serve as the intermediary for the project," exclaimed Raul. "That's what the meeting was for," said Raul. Agitation was now in his voice as he cleared his throat. "To get any and all input that you may have pertaining to this," he stated. "What are you so afraid of Amp?" He asked.

Tate looked Raul in the eye and replied, "Too fear means to give power too." He clinched his teeth. "I fear no man," said Tate.

Raul replied, "Let's not get philosophical. It just seems that you're kind of skittish about this whole thing that's all."

Tate said, "Let me ask a serious question. It has been a rumor among black elites of an organization known as the Non-Group, are you apart of this?"

Raul paused for a moment and replied, "No but take some friendly advice Tate, beware of the toes you step on." With that remark Raul exited the room leaving Tate to ponder in his own thoughts.

Tate was aware that sometime in the twentieth century a group of elitist mostly Caucasians and Hispanics banded together to dictate county political operations. This group was a terror to any that stood in the way of its agenda economically or politically. Meetings were generally conducted by way of monthly dinners. They were largely organized in the way the current chamber of commerce business meetings are conducted. Tate knew to take Raul's veiled threat very seriously for their most notable attack was done by character assassination.

Tate realized that he would have to be conscience of all his actions from now on out to avoid from getting caught up. He would have to accomplish duties better than average and leave no loose ends. Tate was concerned about his protégé Terrence Kemp, who had been approached by a member of this consortium in the way of Chris Mogoya. Tate was of the resolve that he would try to provide guidance to Terrence to the best of his ability. However, in politics ultimately you are on your own and must play whatever hand you're dealt. Tate was unaware of the nature of the relationship Terrence had with Chris. Tate would not risk his neck for anyone for the sake of ignorance on the part of naivety in the political arena.

Black politicians in South Florida are reduced to "yes massa" politics and if you want to get anything accomplished for your disenfranchised poor and minority constituents you must play ball with the big boys. Tate knew the consequence for standing against the political flow of things is to invite terrible wrath upon one's head. Many black politicians that came before Tate who got wise to the game were targeted for elimination.

***

On a muggy day under the blazing South Florida sun Miami's most powerful and influential political figures joined developer Chris Mogoya on a blighted track of land in Downtown Miami. They stood in the middle of a shade less lot donning shovels and silver hardhats. Tate peered through tinted windows as he rode by the scene with his car windows wound up tight. The A/C cooled the interior of the car as they rolled up in the direction of the gathering. "Keep driving, I'm not staying for this," he said to Ray from the back seat. The group was posing for pictures in front of a large lithograph portraying state-of-the art casino buildings, tidy lawns and street lined palm trees. "Take me by Terrence's place," Tate barked again from the back seat.

Ray maneuvered the black Cadillac through the streets towards the Overtown Community Center. Ray pulled a cigarette from his pocket and attempted to light it. Tate said, "Ray, how many times have I told you no smoking while I am in the back seat of this car." Ray with the cigarette dangling between his lips replied, "Right boss," as he slipped the cigarette behind his ear and put the lighter away. Tate thought to himself, he would chat with Terrence and get his impression of today's ground breaking events, regarding the down town casino development. He also needed to get Terrence's impression on this

Mogoya fella. Terrence was an ambitious individual and Tate knew that Mogoya could hook him with a good pitch.

The black Cadillac pulled up to the front of the center and Tate hoped out. He had shown up unannounced but was met at the building door by Terrence. "Amp I didn't know you were stopping by, I'm headed to a meeting downtown."

Tate replied, "Cool I'll walk you to your car."

Terrence with an incredulous look, replied, "Sure."

As they strode to Terrence's Benz Tate asked, "What do you think of Chris Mogoya's development plan?"

"If it helps the local community I am all for it," said Terrence. He fumbled in his pant pocket for his keys.

"Well that remains to be seen," said Tate, "and didn't he pledged to build housing units near your vicinity," Tate asked? He tried to mask the sarcasm in his voice.

"Yes," replied Terrence, "but it's your district Amp. I don't see why you are making such a deal about this," exclaimed Terrence. Pointing toward the car with his key in hand he remotely opened his car door.

"Listen I support economic and development in the community but let's not sell our souls on this," Said Tate. "Be careful with the guy Terrence, he is in bed with Raul and you know what that means," Said Tate.

"I know the process Amp," said Terrence. "I am willing to roll the dice on this one," he said as he jumped in his car. Tate was uneasy with Terrence's response but he realized the point. Something was happening to start development in the community.

Ray pulled the Cadillac around and picked Tate up after Terrence sped off in his sport edition Mercedes Benz. "Should we follow him," asked Ray.

"Naw, forget about it," replied Tate.

Tate envisioned harnessing a united community movement based on ballot generated economic approval process of government expenditures. This essentially would put the power of funds approval in the hands of the people leaving the appointed representatives to serve more in a technical role of budget allocations. Tate knew class division in the black community was apparent and in relation to politics could breed corruption. Tate, Terrence and other black officials represented the product of a post-civil rights movement in the United

States of America. The relationship between race, class and politics had been transformed in the last 40 years since the movement. Ray thought to himself Terrence likely had his own internal conflict; in order for progress relations had to be cultivated with the unfavorable that wield undisputed power in this county.

Within Tate's district about three decades ago racial tensions erupted in a frenzy of violence after the acquittal of four white police officers charged with the beating death of an unarmed black insurance salesman. In the aftermath of the May 1980 riot, many businesses packed up and moved to the suburbs. This movement took thousands of inner city jobs and middle class working people with it. Local politicians seeking to reverse the trend experimented with many economic plans to entice businesses back to the area.

***

Tate was driven back to the office by Ray and upon entering was handed a note by his secretary. Tate opened it and read the note aloud, "Call me at this number when you get a moment 3057779311. R.W." Tate shoved the note into his pocket and walked into his office. His mind was still swirling with Raul, the developer and Terrence. As he shuffled through some papers he thought to himself who the hell is R.W.?

The Music Industry

Nestled in an office park located on south beach sat the headquarters for Light Star Entertainment. Tate was looking forward to the meeting with Jeremy and Lisa Shilling for weeks about finalizing the group's contracts. Tate walked through the glass doors into the crowded music filled lobby. The lobby was very spacious with a huge company seal centered on the middle of the marble floor. A huge stone desk sat in the back of the lobby flanked by armed private plain clothes security guards. Two glass plated elevators ran along the back lobby wall on the right and left sides of the stone desk. The lobby was sparsely decorated with leather sofa sets and glass top tables with steel sitting chairs. There was a photographer shooting still shots of a group of young women modeling on the sitting chairs. A group of young men sat in an area behind them along the wall on the leather sofa's chatting loudly about sports.

"Can I help you Sir," one of the plain clothes guard asked as Tate walked up to the desk.

"I'm Anthony Tate I was scheduled for a ten O'clock meeting with Ms. Shilling," Tate replied as he looked around the lobby.

The guard seated behind the desk checked a log and gave Tate a nod. The guard standing motioned to the elevator on the right; "take it to the penthouse," he instructed.

Tate stepped from the elevator directly into the office of Lisa Shilling, "Come in commissioner glad you made it," she exclaimed. Lisa's office encompassed the entire top floor of the building with a working bathroom in the rear. The furniture in the office consisted of Pininfarina designed office chairs, ergonomic designed desks and hi-tech audio video systems. Lisa was sitting on a large circular leather sofa with a remote in hand and to the left of her sat Jeremy. A music video was playing on a movie size plasma screen on an adjacent wall. "Have a seat commissioner we were just looking over some videos that the group has made," she said.

No problem," Tate replied, "I have cleared my schedule for this meeting I have all the time in the world."

Jeremy nodded in Tate's direction and gave him a thumbs up sign. Tate looked around Lisa's office and thought to himself this was a far different comparison from his government cookie cut public office space. It made him realize the different mission objectives of private and public organizational functions.

Lisa placed a call on her desk phone and the group members of Haze stepped off the elevator into her office a couple of minutes later. Lisa presented the record label contracts and the group members signed with no hesitation through the assurance of Jeremy. Tate took notice of the process of contracting in relation to the music business. It was very different from the public contracting process of local or city government in procurement of services. Tate looked over a copy of the contract and noticed a number of interesting points in it. The group signed with Jeremy as an alternate member and a hundred thousand dollar advance had been documented.

Copyrights would be owned by the record company until the artists stopped performing as a group then all would proportionally revert back to the members. Lastly royalties would be set in relation to initial records sales and renegotiation rights of royalties would be deemed waived upon preference of dollar advance.

Tate looked up from the contract and peered around the room. The group members of haze were ecstatic about signing the deal and Jeremy was all smiles. Tate looked at Lisa and she said, "Commissioner the company recognizes you as manager of the group haze and I will meet with you separately to discuss authorizations for per diem and budget expenses." Tate was well adept to the workings of the business process as it is not too far removed from that of the political process. "Good deal," Tate replied he turned to Jeremy, "come by the shop later so we can chat," he said. As Tate rose to leave he congratulated the group with handshakes and high fives on the way to the elevator.

Tate knew that a couple of Jeremy's friends had an interest in the music group and it was rumored in the streets that they invested monetarily. Mammoth was rumored to be assigned to a soon to be created record label of Haze for the purpose of bringing investors in as corporate owners. Tate was well connected to the community and was privileged to such outside information. Tate was acquainted with the elders of the community and their kids. There was a certain type of loyalty Tate garnered as being the commissioner of the district. Tate wanted to level with Jeremy and he would do it in a place that Jeremy would be at ease which is the Barbershop.

***

Tate arrived at the barbershop on Beale Street and stopped to put out his stogie before he pulled open the door.

"What's up Amp," a voice said from the street, it was Jeremy.

Tate slipped the cigar into his pocket. "Hey Jeremy I want to talk with you about getting things clear about my deal with you and the group," said Tate. "I think it's great the deal went through but the contract is questionable in my eyes and I didn't see anything pertaining to our agreement." The door of the barbershop pushed open as a customer stepped out exiting the shop.

"Listen Amp," said Jeremy as he pulled him aside. "Our agreement is concrete as long as I have anything to do with it. We gonna get paid man, calm yourself down," said Jeremy. "Lisa made it clear that she was signing the group and anything else was largely the priority of the group unless we opted for corporate management."

"And another thing," said Tate. "What's the deal with Lisa she seems to have a lot of say in group activities."

"It's nothing," replied Jeremy. "She is just looking out for her investment that's all. "Listen Amp I have a couple of investors and I need you as my manager to go see them at this address," said Jeremy. He handed Tate a note that read, *Bronson House 2100 Riverside Street.* "When you do this give me a call," said Jeremy as he pulled the door open to the barber shop and disappeared inside. Tate stood on the sidewalk under the brisling South Florida sun with the note grasped in his hand.

"I got to make a call," Tate said aloud to himself "and I know just who to call on this."

***

An SUV sat and idled on the curb at Commissioner Tate's residence behind the driver's side wheel sat Ray Sutter. He sat with the driver's side window and his arm hung out as he smoked cherry scented tobacco cigars. Tate Jumped in the back of the vehicle and was instantly irritated with the smell of the heavy aroma of the cigar. "Ray," he said, "next time stand outside the car when you smoke those cheap cigars."

"No problem boss," Ray replied with a chuckle. "We can't all smoke the best like you big ballers and shot callers," he remarked. Tate reached over the back seat and handed Ray the note Jeremy gave to him earlier.

"Put this address into the navigation system and punch it I have a full schedule today and want to get done ASAP," he said. The SUV pulled up at the address on Riverside Street both Tate and Ray approached the front door of a two story brownstone. The door swung open before they could knock and in front of them stood a young woman with pigtails in her hair.

"Did Jeremy send you guys she asked in a high pitched voice?" "Yeah," replied Tate. She handed Tate a folded brown paper bag wrapped in gray electrical tape and closed the door. Tate and Ray looked at each other shrugging their shoulders, "let's get out of here boss," Ray replied. As the SUV pulled up the block Tate gave Jeremy a call on the cell phone, "Hey I got that package for you," said Tate into the receiver.

"Great bring it by the studio," said the voice from the other end of the receiver. Tate felt uneasy about being in the situation of running errands for any person let alone that of a wannabe rapper. Many politicians fall prey the vices of others because of money. Tate had seen this in many situations and as a black politician he tried hard to dodge such situations because his kind falls harder.

The SUV pulled into the parking lot of the studio, Tate nudged Ray, "Take this up to Jeremy," he said as he handed the package to Ray, "and have him give me a call."

"No problem," Ray replied and stepped from the SUV. Ray was uncertain what was in the package but common sense would lead him to suspect it was money. If it was money why would Jeremy, put him in the quandary of picking it up Tate thought to himself. Tate's phone ran and it was Jeremy, "Hey I sent your consulting fee for the contracts with Ray, I will 1099 you later," he said with a laugh before he hung up the call.

Ray hopped in the car ten minutes later and pulled off. Tate asked, "How is Jeremy?"

Ray remarked, "Good boss." Tate watched as Ray put an envelope in the arm rest compartment of the vehicle. They rode in silence for a couple of minutes before either spoke.

"Boss I'm stopping here at this café for some Cuban Coffee," said Ray.

"No problem, bring me a shot," replied Tate. Ray got out and entered the Café as he disappeared into the establishment Tate opened the armrest and took out the envelope. It contained ten grand in crisp one hundred dollar bills wrapped in large rubber bands. Tate placed the envelope in his briefcase and sat back with a sigh, I hope this contract works out in my favor he thought to himself as he viewed Ray headed back to the car.

Tate desired to be an entrepreneur and this business venture could put him on the track to attaining such a dream. Most politicians are self sufficient financial citizens and the office they hold are not their only job. Tate saw himself as a career politician and his only job was as a selfless public servant to the district. In his opinion those with many occupations and business ventures fall prey to corruption. Tate detested corruption and believed it violated the most basic principle in regard to republicanism. Corruption is the cost of living under a government structure built in and for the 19th century. Tate believed corruption was especially detrimental to the black politician because of the sliding scale associated with judgment.

"Where too boss?" Ray inquired as he got back into the car.

Tate paused for a moment, "take me to the studio," he replied while still in thought.

"Everything alright?" Ray asked while he glanced in the rearview mirror.

"Good Ray Good, Say turn the radio to Rushing99," said Tate.

Ray leaned over and switched the radio on to the station. Haze was on air giving an interview about their newly released single. "You think this Hip Hop group music is going to be hit boss," Ray asked. "I hope so Ray I am taking a gamble in investing in this thing.

I'm placing my name and credibility on the line here," replied Tate. "Jeremy seems to have a handle on the group but I'm not sure he knows what he is getting into with Lisa," Tate said. "The music business is just that a business and like politics you play to win," Tate said.

Ray replied, "Well I want you to know boss that I got your back." "It's a dirty game, that I know," said Ray. "I also know people and from what I have heard about this Lisa Shilling she is a shark." Tate leaned toward the tinted window of the SUV and looked out at the passing scenery of traffic.

"Well I know a thing or two about sharks Ray," Tate replied, "I swim with them every day." "My Dad had a saying," said Tate. "Sometimes it's worse to win a fight than to lose." The SUV glided through traffic weaving in and out under the heat of

102

the South Florida sun as the radio blared. Haze wrapped up there interview session with the local Disk Jockey and introduced the upcoming spin for their hottest single. Ray adjusted the climate temperature in the truck then reached over and switched the radio off.

Tate realized he had to put more time into his artist management role, if he was to be successful. He did realize he would serve as a representative of a voice, to a culture within the music industry which associates the genre as a fad more or less. Tate also could see the link between rap artists and the poor. The rapper and a poor resident in the district both can relate to being oppressed by the larger society. Tate realized as a representative in his district he was the voice of those that had no voice individually. He could see how rappers could equate their art form to his role as being a voice for the unheard.

Tate reached his office around noon and was dropped off by Ray with instructions to pick him up later for a meeting downtown. Tate thought further on the comparisons of the music industry and politics. He realized in making a living in both careers they are set up in a way to mirror the larger capitalist society. The larger society seeks to benefit and maintain itself, the people on top and their culture. Capitalism by its very nature benefits and sustains the person above more than the person below. In the real world, the object of the game is to keep control where it is. Those in power know that if someone or something is perceived as a threat, you control it, silence it or eliminate it. In the greater society of the political system efforts at cohesiveness are often times hindered, images of progress perverted, thoughts of revolution or rebellion quelled and voices of discontent are silenced. If silencing does not work than it must be modified until it can safely be perceived, packaged and presented effectively.

The pace and priorities within the music industry mirror those of the political systems of America. As in politics power comes down to the issue of control, if control is not feasible it'll be made distasteful or unacceptable to the majority of society thereby justifying removal. Tate sat behind his desk in thought and realized that he ultimately wanted to do the will of the people in all things. He initially saw his progression in politics as a career and all other endeavors as a means to an end. He truly realized at this point in his life he could become more than his own ambition and was anxious

***

Tate began to prep for his meeting and jotted down a couple of notes to remind him of who was to be present. The meeting was to be held at a public library in his district concerning neighborhood crime. The chief of police was scheduled to be present along with the precinct captain and other resource officers. Tate had never personally met the chief and was interested in how the community viewed his policies. Crime had always been an issue in the community with past drug related shootings involving innocent youth and bystander's. Many media outlets also felt the whole hip hop or rap culture stimulates black on black crime. Tate knew that many black youth in his district saw hip hop as a way out of poverty.

The meeting began with the pledge of allegiance and the opening announcement came from a community board member. Tate sat listening as one by one forum attendees protested against police brutality. Tate eyed the room and finally caught site of the Chief seated on the end of the front row in the resident audience. The Chief was in full police regalia with all the trimmings of a military styled uniform. Tate rose stating, "I think the Chief should address all issues relating to crime in the community." Tate motioned toward the Chief to address the residents, the Chief in his full service police uniform glittered under the forum lights with all sorts of service medals he earned during his career in law enforcement. He spoke in a baritone voice stating, "I would like to thank the commissioner for his foresight and police brutality will be investigated on a case by case basis as it relates to the complaints." There was a subdued belittle response from the crowd. The Chief continued, "The issue of crime is of major concern and studies have suggested cultural influences such as music and gang activity are key in combating the problem."

Tate listened with interest to the Chief's words and watched the response of the residents in response to the comments stated. Tate could see that the Chief's approach to the issue of community wellbeing and police law enforcement would not go smoothly with residents. The approach was insensitive to the vast majority of residents and Tate knew that he would have to step in at some point to curtail the problem.

Many city cops take off duty assignments in music related after hour jobs especially in hip hop venues throughout the city. Tate thought to himself such negative talk about the influence of music in crime would seek to unhinge the Chief's administration. After the Chief's speech he thanked the residents for their cooperation and support and was seated. The meeting ended with all the attending officials chatting briefly in the lobby.

Tate stood chatting with a constituent when he was approached by the Chief, "finally our paths have crossed commissioner." The Chief extended his hand and Tate shook it with a firm grip.

"Good to meet you Chief, interesting speech there," Tate replied.

Still grasping Tate's hand the Chief leaned close saying between a clinched toothy smile, "Do you think it's wise doing business in this rap music business thing?"

Tate realized that the Chief was in his business and was apparently using city resources to obtain information about him. Tate was a commissioner indirectly the Chief's boss. Tate slapped the Chief on the back replying with a wide smile, "Get your hands out of my pocket Chief." With that remark Tate turned and headed for the exit leaving the Chief with a confused look on his face. Tate on occasion enjoyed using various cultural vernaculars to perplex individuals soliciting a certain response from him. He realized that it was beneficial in illustrating a puzzling scenario when relaying the incident to others. This tactic basically left the Chief without cause to tell the response of his inquiry to others.

***

Tate sat at his desk in city hall thinking over the events that happened at the community center the night before. He picked up his phone and made a call to the police union president and inquired about the Chief's intent related to off duty police work assignments. Tate hung up the phone receiver and reared back in his chair. The Chief would surely face retaliation if he continued to make veiled suggestion changes related to off duty work assignments of the lower tier law enforcement officer. Tate thought the Chief to be an idiot if he continued in this direction which would surely erode his power base within the department with rank and file personnel. Tate believed that the Chief's own covetousness of a black man making real money would cause his own downfall.

"Some people just don't know when to let go," Said Tate aloud with a chuckle. Power struggles occur at every instant in the political fray of government and being a black official puts one at an obvious disadvantage which Tate was well aware of.

Tate's secretary walked into his office, "I'm sorry commissioner did you call for me?"

"Sure," Tate replied, "I will be out of the office in the field for the rest of the day. Hold all my calls."

"Will do commissioner," she replied with a smile, satisfied that she would have the office to herself.

Tate was a man of ambition and he wanted to get the most out of the opportunity of managing Jeremy and the group. He needed information and was interested in arranging a meeting with Lisa Shilling. However, he was hesitant in meeting without Jeremy and unsure how to approach the dilemma he faced. Tate placed a call to Ray. "Meet me out front," he said before he hung up the phone.

Tate walked out of City Hall the bright sun blazed as he jumped into the back of the waiting car.

"Where to boss," Ray inquired.

"Let's go by the label," Tate replied. Tate thought to himself he would pop up unannounced and say that he was the neighborhood and decided to stop in. That would give the notion that it was not a pre-planned meeting. Tate's SUV pulled up to the front entrance of Light Star Entertainment and he jumped out entering the building. He encountered the burly guards in the lobby, "I'm here to see Ms. Shilling," he said.

A guard phoned Lisa's office, "Someone will be done to meet you," the guard replied. Tate stood with his hands in his suit pockets and looked about the lobby as he waited deep in thought. He wondered how he could question Lisa about the

113

entertainment business without seeming like a novice. If Lisa realized that he's not as sophisticated as he let own about the business he could be placed at a disadvantage in future business dealings. The elevator doors opened to the lobby and a young woman with shoulder length curly hair stepped out. She walked toward Tate extending her hand. "Hello commissioner I'm Ms. Shilling's secretary," she said in melodic voice. Tate was smitten by the young women's aura. "She's out for today but I will be happy to assist you," she said.

Tate smoothly replied, "I was here to take Lisa to lunch and show her some of the district but I will be honored if you could fill in for her."

"Let's go!" replied Ms. Shilling's secretary.

***

Tate sat in Dora's Rib Emporium with Lisa Shilling's secretary talking about his district and his years of public service. The restaurant was filled with people and the servers hurried about helping the patrons. The Rib place was located in Tate's district. A stand-alone Art Deco styled building; it was an established landmark of the community.

"Commissioner did you know that I won you in your fund raising raffle," stated the secretary demurely.

"Really," replied Tate in his most surprised expression.

"You're just full of surprises, aren't you," he jested.

"How long have you worked with Lisa?" he asked.

She answered, "I have worked with her for only a couple of months, but my uncle's a producer and I have been in the business all my life."

Finally Tate thought to himself someone with the inside knowledge of the business. Tate sat across the table admiring the young woman's youth and experience as she discussed her family's history in the music business. "As you know I manage a group and I would love it if you could come down to the studio some time and meet them," stated Tate.

She replied, "I would love too, just let me know when!" "Great!" Exclaimed Tate, "I am famished let's get an order of ribs, they're the best in the city here," said Tate.

***

Jeremy sat in the studio checking messages on his smart phone. He stopped at the last message on his phone and dialed the number for it. "Amp!" he yelled into his Bluetooth. "We need to meet regarding some business," said Jeremy. "Cool," he said before ending the call.

Jeremy's phone rang, "Yeah," he answered. "I've been waiting here in the studio for a half hour now." He said into the phone. "Man where you at?" Jeremy sat up. "The docks," he replied. "Man I told you not there." Jeremy stood up and paced the room. "Fine, be there in a minute," he said as he ended the call.

Jeremy took the service elevator down to the garage and jumped in his lime green Chevy Impala punching the gas. The 22 inch tires spun and made a screeching sound on the slick floor of the parking area. Jeremy headed to the Port of Miami, his phone rang again and he ignored it as he ran a stop light.

He pulled his car into the port's parking area and was met by his pal who worked as a deck hand on one of the ships. His pal hopped in the car placing a huge duffle bag in the back seat. Jeremy lit a Newport took a couple of puffs and passed it to his pal as he pulled out of port parking. A black Escalade truck pulled in front of Jeremy's car blocking his exit and then a white charger pulled in behind him. Jeremy gripped the steering wheel tight as the blood ran from his hands and slumped his head down hitting the backside of his white blood drained knuckles. "Damn!"

Jeremy and the Federals

Tate sat in the barber's chair and clicked through the television channels as he received a haircut from his barber. He lounged comfortably but was a little perturbed that Jeremy had not contacted him. The time was twelve-noon, the shop was full of customers who milled around for the next available chair to open.

Tate said to his barber Movay, "I have been trying to reach Jeremy and he has not been in place lately." The clippers buzzed in his ear as Movay tapered his hairline.

Movay replied, "You know Jeremy, he always into something, no telling what he's up to." Tate continued to flip through the channels and stopped when he saw a breaking news story.

The news lady at the scene reported, "Breaking news of huge drug bust at the Port of Miami, men get caught with bricks of dope from freighter."

***

Jeremy sat in a sunlight filled bay behind a gated fence and felt a bit nervous because he had never really been arrested for a crime. Two men entered the bay dressed in khaki pants and black polo shirts.

The first man spoke, "Mr. Coons you're looking at a conspiracy charge that's going to be hard to beat unless you cooperate with us."

Jeremy looked the man in the eyes, "first who are you and cooperate how," he replied.

"That's what I want to hear," said the second man. "We represent the United States D.E.A. and we have been conducting an investigation in which you may be able to assist us in closing."

Jeremy looked around the bay wondering why he had not been led away to lock up with his pal, he hung his head in disbelief. Tate walked out of the barber's thinking about the news report of the bust that occurred on the port. He had felt relief that it had not happened in his district and the port was well out of his jurisdiction. The port was a gateway to the Caribbean and other third world countries to include Columbia. Cocaine shipments flowed through those corridors to Miami in the early eighties and nineties solidifying Miami as the cocaine capital of the south. Many families in Tate's district had ties in other countries and many of the city's youth utilize such an advantage in organizing criminal shipments of illegal contraband. Tate thought of the many criminal elements of the society and how they influence the functions of everyday living. With high unemployment rates and the pressure of success that dictates status in American society many turn down the detrimental path of crime.

***

Jeremy sat alone at the studio the next morning in total silence pondering his predicament and weighing his options. The only reason he was released was conditioned on his cooperation with the feds. He wondered was this condition a blanket one or were they setting up something big which would include him in some way. He was completely clueless on the matter; however he was happy to not have been formerly charged. He decided to play the situation down and remain silent about the whole

incident. He looked down at his cell phone; there

were three missed calls from Tate and two voice

messages. He decided he would give Lisa a call, Tate

would have to wait he thought aloud to himself as he

dialed Lisa up.

"Lisa," said Jeremy into the speaker phone, "I

need to meet with you ASAP," Jeremy nervously bit

his fingernail which was an old habit of his when he

felt anxious. "Fine," he said ending the call.

Lisa had agreed to meet with him at the record

label headquarters; Jeremy jumped in his ride and

headed out. As Jeremy rounded the garage onto the

street a black SUV pulled up directly in front of his

car blocking the pathway.

Tate bounded out of the truck, "Jeremy, I have been trying to contact you for days now," he said. "What's going on?"

Jeremy replied, "Hey Amp, yeah I have some personal issues I am dealing with."

Tate looked Jeremy over and asked, "Yeah ok, when can we start up marketing plans for the boys?"

Jeremy replied, "I have a couple ideas that I'm playing with let me get back to you later and we can schedule a time to meet to get things rolling."

"Alright Jeremy," said Tate as he hopped back in the black SUV and pulled out of the garage.

"Everything on the up and up boss?" asked Ray as he wheeled the SUV down the winding Miami streets.

"Not sure Ray," replied Tate, "Jeremy has been missing in action lately and I don't know what's going on with him." Tate knew that Jeremy was attuned to the street life of Miami and had friends that seemed a bit shady. Tate did not want anything to distract Jeremy from the business of music and promoting the best interest of the group.

"Do you want me to follow him and keep an eye out boss?" said Ray.

"Forget about it." said Tate. He gazed out the window and wondered where Jeremy was going off to in such a rush. Tate was not very familiar personally with the members of the rap group crew and had the intuition that he should establish some type of rapport with his business interests.

"You know what," he remarked to Ray, "I have not been spending much time with the group to get to know the guys."

"Yeah, you know you're about old enough to be their father," said Ray.

"Turn around, let's go back to the studio," said Tate.

"Fine," said Ray as he wheeled the SUV around.

***

The studio was now filled with music and the group Haze had their entourage in the lobby while they laid a voice over on a new track for a single. Tate walked in and they greeted him with a nod as they continued with their work. It was awkward to Tate that the entire music making process has developed into a mostly computerized process. Tate watched as the engineer worked the dials and volume controls on the sound board. The group members of Haze took turns going into the sound booth to complete production of one of their feature songs. Tate engaged one of the group members in conversation as he came out of the booth, "Hey how long will it take you guys to do a whole album to put out for distribution?"

"Just let us know and we can get it together," the young man replied. "We have volumes of work." He said. Tate thought to himself with a ready available product more time could be put into marketing as opposed to production. Tate would have to review the label contract to determine the budget for marketing and other related costs for getting the music out to the public. He also would need to get together with Jeremy to organize a release party for Haze. Another member was entering the booth to record when Tate stopped him. "Would you guys appreciate a release party for the group?" Tate asked.

"We're always open for a good party," the group member replied as he hurried into the booth. Tate hung out in the studio with the group for a couple of hours and learned that some of the members were from Haitian and Cuban backgrounds. Their families had relocated to the United States of America for a better life. The group Haze represented the diverse society of the City of Miami and that fact was displayed in their music.

The Secretary

Tate sat in a white straight back chair while a cigar dangled from his lips, "Damn it Ray, give me a hand," he said. As he struggled with his line, he jerked back and reeled his graphite rod to tighten the line hoping to hook his catch. The ocean water splashed up against the yacht as the current drifted to and fro in the sunny afternoon. Tate fished as a kid with his father but never really was good at catching the big fish.

"Pull it in boss, you got it," said Ray as he adjusted his sunglasses. "I once caught a 15lb Snapper off the Florida Bay, I did it the old Macedonian way," Ray exclaimed. "I fastened a piece of crimson red wool onto my hook, took two cock feathers and dropped it in the water." Ray's glass lens sparkled in the sunlight. "Man I fought with that fish on my line for 7 minutes and he was madder than hell but I reeled it in." Tate placed his foot on the back wall of the vessel and continued to reel while yoking the rod. Most of the better fishing spots were located off the shore of Port Everglades. Biscayne Bay seemed especially active today with schools of fish prevalent in the waters. Tate had read many Florida Sportsman Magazines and watched many T.V. episodes of Fishing with Roland Martin. It was espoused prevention against line twist and line tensions are essential in bringing up the big fish. With one final thrust Tate pulled the big fish into the boat. The yacht cruised back into the harbor with a slow listless effort and the engines purred with a low quiet murmur. Tate knew of many lobbyist and they clamored to provide outings to elected officials in order to bend their ear for certain issues of corporate concern. Freedom Boat Club was a well-known club in Tate's district and they often had fundraisers on his behalf. As the boat docked at the Marina the crew joked with Tate about landing his 12lb swordfish.

"Nice catch commissioner," said the secretary from Lisa Shilling's office.

"Excuse me," said Tate to a crew member as he finished posing for a picture with the fish. Tate walked towards the secretary; she had a pair of designer Gucci sunglasses on and a floppy stray hat covering her head. Her bathing suit was still wet from her day out at sea, "What are you doing here?" Tate asked with a broad smile.

"Both business and pleasure," she replied. "One of our artists had a video shoot out near cove's bay and I volunteered to help in the project."

Tate looked her over and replied, "You look totally different outside the office setting." She pulled her sunglasses down to the tip of her nose and said, "Is that a good or bad thing?"

"It's totally good!" Tate said as he glanced around the peer. "So where is your entourage?" Tate asked.

She replied, "Oh most of them have left, I saw you over here and thought I would say hello."

Tate thought to himself this would be a great time to learn more about Light Star Entertainment. "Have you heard anything related to the group Haze that I manage," he asked.

She replied "I have not heard anything about the group Haze."

"I would love to do lunch with you if you are available?" Tate asked. "What's your schedule looking like today?" He inquired.

She said, "lets meet in about two hours I have a couple of things to take care of back at the office."

"Great, we can meet over at Joe's off Ocean Drive and 1st," Tate replied.

"Ok, I know the place," The secretary replied.

Ray stumbled off the yacht with a cooler and another package under his arm. With a cigarette that dangled from his lips he asked, "You ready boss?" With a smile he motioned to Ray to take the things to the car. Ray struggled with the packages but made his way down the dock.

Hold on Ray," said Tate. He walked over towards Ray took the cooler from under his arm opened it and took out something wrapped in foil. "Thanks Ray," Tate replied as he walked toward the secretary. "Here," he told her extending his hand. "Enjoy the catch." It was a filleted swordfish brisket.

She said, "Thanks you're the consummate gentlemen." She than leaned into Tate and gave him a slight hug. Tate could smell the soft scent of her body wash cologne.

"Now there is an art to cooking this kind of fish," Tate said. "It has to marinate just right with onions, lemon and salt." Tate grabbed her hand, "Then sautéed in a light olive oil based broth."

She took her hand out of his and said, "I tell you what, why don't we do lunch at this address."

She took a pen from her beach bag and wrote down an address on a slip of white paper and handed it to Tate.

"Cool I will be there with bells on!" Tate exclaimed.

She chuckled and looked Tate in the eyes, "You are so crazy." She turned and walked down the dock disappearing into a crowd of people who disembarked from a nearby boat. Tate slid the address into his pant pocket and looked around for Ray.

***

The glass door of a high rise condominium was slightly ajar as wicker blinds rapped gently against the inner door frame from the blower of the air conditioner. Two figures are in bed silhouetted by silk curtains which frame the four sides of the canopy.

The male silhouette kissed the female and the sound of wet smooches could be heard. They rolled onto the left side of the bed and the female silhouette slipped on top and mounted the male. Low moans of ecstasy could be heard throughout the room as the female bobbed up and down as she gyrated ferociously. The male's silhouetted toes curled and flinched as the pace of the female silhouette increased. The sound of flesh slapped against another was heard as it maintained a steady tempo. A female voice lets out a soft moan "yes baby," she said and the sound slowed in pace. The male silhouette flipped her on her back then turned her on her stomach. He then twisted a hand full of her hair in hand and mounted her from behind. She grinded up against his body her wide hips slapped against his thighs. The flesh sound continued with velocity as the male silhouette went to and fro as if like a jack hammer in concrete. The male

voice let out a prolonged moan as his pace slowed

and the female flopped belly first on the bed.

Second half; the male silhouette stood as he

straddled the bed he lifted the female with her crotch

in his face and his in hers they suckled each other

erotically. Her moans rose and fell as tongue

flickered sounds emanated from the male silhouette.

She prodded and pulled her head went back and

forth in a locomotive type movement. The male

moaned and with slightly bent knees tried to

maintain balance while he straddled the bed. She

wrapped her arms around his legs which helped to

maintain balance and sustain a couple more minutes

of pleasure. The weight of the position was too much

to bear for the male silhouette and they tumble to the

bed. The two figures lay intertwined with each other

and kissed and rolled around the bed. The male rolled on top and pumped in an up and down motion on the female. She moaned as she wrapped her legs around his waist which locked him into position as he caressed her breast. The male silhouette stiffened and with a loud moan grabbed the female and held her tight. They lay and play fought both giggled as the bed canopy shook from their playful romp.

Jeremy's Bribes and the Permits/Empowerment Trust

Tate sat in the office and reviewed loads of paperwork that had accumulated over a week's time span. He hated tedious work and wished for an excuse to avoid his present task. His secretary buzzed him on the intercom, "commissioner there is an individual here to meet with you, his name is Jeremy," she said. Tate paused shuffled some papers and thought to himself why would Jeremy want to meet him at the office.

Tate replied, "Wait fifteen minutes and send him in."

"Yes" sir she replied. The sound of the intercom buzzed as she clicked off.

As commission chair of the entertainment permitting division Tate's duties can become quite routine and complex. Companies that shoot movies, music videos, commercials, etc. must file permit applications with the commission's chair office. Tate sat in his office to review submitted applications as well as make notes to himself regarding decisions.

Jeremy entered the office, "What a pleasant surprise," said Tate as he stood to shake Jeremy's hand. "Have a seat sir," Said Tate motioning to a chair in front of his desk. "What can I do you for?" Tate asked.

"Let's get right to it Amp," Jeremy said as he positioned himself in the chair. "I have some friends that are looking to do some video shoots downtown."

Jeremy clasped his hands together. "What do I need to do to help them get permits to set up shop?" Tate rocked by in his chair and doodled on a nearby pad as he did on occasion.

"Jeremy to be straight with you they would need a million dollar insurance coverage plan and of course, a disclaimer filled out by the company to cover the city in case of incidentals." Tate replied.

"The guys I am working with don't have a million dollar insurance plan," he said. "They are well known in the music and video industry and have more of a startup company." Tate listened and continued to doodle. "They have been building their brand for years now and are willing to pay to play," said Jeremy.

Tate stood and walked over toward the office window, "I hear what you are saying Jeremy and I will do what I can," said Tate. "With organizations in your case I refer them to a fellow colleague, Terrence Kemp; I think you know each other."

"Yeah," said Jeremy, "I know him from the neighborhood."

Tate continued, "I will work on getting the paper work ready and you let your friends know to have their business in order." Jeremy rose from his chair and walked toward the door.

"Thanks Amp," "I will get on the ball with this and let you know the outcome," he said as he exited the room. Tate stood and peered out the window still in his thoughts, Jeremy showed up unexpectedly with a money making business proposal. While he should've been more predisposed with the welfare of the group, he was doing deals for some other folks. Tate thought the whole exchange funny and was surprised Jeremy showed up to the office unannounced.

Tate decided to give Terrence a call and let him know about Jeremy. Terence had coordinated video shoots before on referral from Tate and because of his position had insider knowledge of the more desirable locations in Miami. Tate explained the arrangement with Terrence of Jeremy's situation and Terrence went with it. Tate being Terrence's senior treated his colleague as a Lieutenant in matters related to the community district. Tate believed such an endeavor would give jobs to the locals and put money in the local small businesses in the community. The Initial video shoots were done for Luke Companies and Benzino production entertainment group. The community district experienced a lot of national attention from the exposure of being a part of the project. Many of the locals had a chance to get work on the sets as janitors, carpenters, electricians and engineers. Tate also believed that working with the entertainment business was good networking. He also believed Terrence could also benefit from the exposure.

As Tate discussed the new venture with Terrence he could not help, but relay his doubts and hesitations regarding the deal with Jeremy's business partners. Terrence acknowledged that he would keep an eye out of any suspicious activities. Tate also desired to try and link the Haze rap group in all video features for maximum national exposure. He sought to discuss the matter over with Jeremy, but was unsure if he should link the two business operations together.

He decided he would let the arrangement play out with Jeremy's connection before involving him in other business related interests. Tate ended his discussion with Terrance and arranged for all relevant parties to meet at a later date to work out the loose ends of the proposal. It was made clear that Terrence would bring the business in under his wing; therefore fronting the certificate of liability.

The Empowerment Trust was responsible for economic development within the City of Miami specifically designed to aide development in the Overtown community. Tate sat as head of the Overtown Development Corp which chose what contracts went where in the district.

Raul walked into Tate's Office, "How's it hanging Amp," he bellowed.

"What's the deal?" Tate shot back.

"Just to give you heads up on the Mogoya project," Raul said, "Mogoya has blue prints for a biopharmaceutical park that will span apart of your district as well as my neighboring district downtown." Tate reared back in his chair and listened intently. "His idea is to bring multinational drug companies and prestigious universities in which would develop cutting-edge medical advances."

Tate cleared his throat and replied, "The question is how is this going to benefit the residents?" Raul continued, "With the new advances the public hospitals will be able to provide free healthcare to one-hundred fifty thousand poor residents a year. "

Tate inquired, "How long have you been sold on this thing?"

Raul replied, "From conception and besides fifteen hundred high-paying jobs will flood into the

146

community along with hundreds of millions in investments and tax revenue."

Tate shifted in his seat, "It sounds like you guys have it all planned out," Tate said.

"I just wanted to keep you in the loop," Raul replied as he walked out the office.

Tate walked over to the window and stared out while in thought, this project would be the most dramatic economic development project ever seen in Miami-Dade. It almost sounded too good to be true and Raul was so focused on supporting Magoya's dream. Tate felt very uneasy with the thought of using public funds set aside for the poor to bank roll personal ambitions.

Tate's secretary popped her head in his doorway, "Commissioner I'm on leave for the rest of the day," she said. "Is there anything you need before I go?" She asked.   She waited expecting protest or assignment of another task.

"No, enjoy your evening," Tate replied.

"Goodnight sir," she said closing his door.

Tate gathered his briefcase and walked out of city hall, parked out front Ray stood by the car on his cell phone. "You ready boss?" Ray inquired while he ended his call.

"Let's head home Ray," said Tate.

***

The drive home was peaceful; Tate contemplated his thoughts on the events of the day while Ray fiddled with the car radio. "There are no good Jazz stations when you need them," Ray said under his breath. Tate was greeted with a big hug by Tate Jr. as he entered the house and Cherry had just taken the steaks off the grill for the afternoon dinner.

"How was work babe?" She asked in her chirpy voice.

He liked when she spoke in that tone of voice. He thought it made her sound more effeminate and vulnerable. Tate appreciated a little dominatrix in his sex life.

"Work is always going to be work," Tate bellowed back in an exhaustive voice.

"I think my brain is deep fried," he said as he flopped on the sofa. Cherry continued to prepare dinner while Tate Jr. played at his dad's feet. Tate unwittingly dosed off into dream land.

The next morning Tate stood near the mirror as he dressed for the day and wondered which tie to wear. The Television in his bedroom blared with the morning news turned to the WSVN station network. A young news reporter with stringy blond hair was reporting from the field of a new pharmaceutical park building project.

He stated, "The city's Empowerment Trust is funding $100,000 dollars for Poinciana Park a pharmaceutical park to be built in Metro Miami. Fifteen acres of city owned land will be allotted to developer Chris Mogoya for project development."

Tate stood and watched the news report with a blank expression on his face. A blank check had been practically written by Raul to the developer on the dime of the public. The report cut to an interview of Mogoya, a rotund fella with slick black hair. With a cigar in hand Chris said, "The project will bring in much needed jobs and investments to metro Miami."

As Tate finished dressing and slipped on his coat he felt paper in his pocket. He pulled it out to get a better look at it. There was a number scrawled on it and the initials JW in capital letters. Tate out of instinct called the number on his cell, "Hello Ron Wiggins," the voice said from the other end.

"This is Commissioner Anthony Tate," Tate replied.

"Aw commissioner, I'm glad you called," said Ron. "We spoke briefly at your fundraiser." Tate paused for a moment trying to replay the event in his memory.

"Yes," Tate finally said, "The writer!"

Ron replied, "That's me." "Commissioner I write for Miami News and I am interested in verifying some information with you. "

Tate replied, "As long as they are off the record you can verify with me all day Ron."

"Great I will be in touch," Ron said.

***

Tate reached his office and fond Raul at his doorway, "Good morning commissioner," Tate said shaking Raul's hand.

"Amp here is a project vehicle for your use when performing project related duties," Raul said as he dropped the keys to an Escalade into Tate's hand.

"I have a driver," Tate exclaimed.

"It's just a formality just keep them somewhere handy," Raul replied with irritation in his voice. "Listen we have already begun construction on a five story parking garage and I want you to show up for pictures this afternoon," said Raul.

"Will do," Tate replied as he walked into his office foyer. He greeted the secretary and retreated to his work chamber.

While he sat at his desk Tate received a call from Terrence Kemp, "Good morning commissioner,"

Terrence said with excitement in his voice. "I received a call from Commissioner Sancho informing me that he has access to rent free office space in metro Miami if I was interested

"That's interesting," Tate replied wryly.

"Yeah it is and I took him up on the offer," Terrence replied. "I could use the extra space."

Tate chuckled and replied, "Let's do lunch sometime this week if you have the time."

"Sounds good," Terrence replied hanging up the phone.

Tate thought about the interview of Chris Mogoya on the morning news and noted how Chris seemed sincere in his words of providing jobs for the community. A lot of the land encompassed vacated abandoned buildings and empty lots in the district. Entire areas were blighted due to suburban flight and economic spirals in the housing market. Chris Mogoya seems to be the only viable developer with some kind of revivalists vision for the city. Tate could see Terrence's point of supporting Mogoya in his proposals, but Mogoya would have to be vetted before Tate would give his wavering support. Tate picked up his cell phone and dialed a number.

"Hey boss," the voice said on the other end.

Tate spoke into the receiver, "Be here in an hour, we're headed out to the district and I need you to be in your Sunday's best," he said.

"Great," replied Ray. "I just got this new black suit that I have been dying to wear."

Tate chuckled and replied, "I hope it's a three piece."

"You know it boss, I am from the old school," said Ray. "I only need to stop by and pick up my fedora from the cleaners."

***

Tate arrived at the development sight in downtown Miami and was met by Commissioner Sancho along with other public officials. Reporters milled around the site while workers walked to and fro organizing heavy equipment tools.

"Amp I would like you to meet Chris Magoya," said Raul.

Magoya stepped forward and extended his hand, "finally we get to meet commissioner," he said. Magoya was about two inches taller than Tate with piercing blue eyes and slick back jet black hair. His teeth were perfect and bleach white. He wore a black suit with dark green alligator boots and his tie dark colored matched his boots.

Tate replied, "Finally." He shook Magoya's hand as a reporter snapped a shot of their first introduction to each other. Silver colored hard hats and chrome plated shovels were passed around to all the public officials participating in the project. The representatives posed in front of the heavy earthmovers for photo opts.

Tate thought to himself, he could see why Magoya seems to have instant credibility among Miami's elite political system. He is physically imposing standing at about 6 feet, Inches, with the all American boy looks. He also has the ear of the politically well-connected golden boy of Miami politics Commissioner Raul Sancho. It amazed Tate that black professionals no matter what their pedigree could not simply garner instant creditability as in this instance. Tate was seen as a major player in politics by his professional colleagues and the African American community. If they were able to see behind the curtain and see the real orchestrators it certainly would be a horrifying experience. Tate thought to himself, he would certainly have to be conscious of his political maneuverings.

The lavish ground breaking ceremony generated a huge media show for the City of Miami politicians. Band wagon participates ranged from community college presidents to local nonprofit Directors. All with intentions to be linked to the project in some form or fashion now or in future endeavors. Tate was sickened by the spectacle and viewed them all as hogs feeding at the trough of big business interests. Magoya certainly had done the home work in lining up local lobbyist, regional area politicians and area chamber of commerce members.

Tate decided to take a ride through his district, after leaving the ground breaking ceremony. He was picked up by Ray before the photo opt had ended. "Are we headed back to the office?" Ray inquired.

"No take me by Terrence's," Tate quipped. As the car rolled down the streets of Overtown the blighted landscape and abandoned buildings were readily noticeable in the community. Ray pulled the black SUV up to the front of the community center as usual and Tate hopped out. "Ray go ahead and park. I will be out in five," Tate said as he strode into the center. Tate walked into Terrence's office.

"Amp, how'd it go?" Terrence asked as he hung up the office phone.

"It was as expected with all the bells and whistles," replied Tate. "I'm quite sure you will be able to catch it on the evening news," Tate said.

"What did you think of Chris Magoya?" asked Terrence.

"The perfect showman from what I can see," Tate replied, "but I am waiting to see if he can stand behind his words," said Tate. Tate walked over to a window in Terrence's office there was a view of the basketball court.

"Give the man a chance," said Terrence eyeing Tate with a wide toothy grin. Tate stood and watched the courts, two kids were shooting hoops.

"I hear what you're saying Terrence," he said in a far-away voice. The larger kid on the court was dribbling the ball between his legs and behind his back showing off his handles. Each time he would shot over the smaller kid he missed the shot. "Let's hope that this thing doesn't turn into one big circus," Tate said turning to facing Terrence.

"Don't worry Amp," Terrence replied. "It will work out in the best interest of the community."

"Let's talk later," Tate replied, "Ray is waiting outside for me," Tate said bolting for the door.

From Terrence's conversation he was firmly in Magoya's camp and supported Raul's agenda for making empowerment zone money available for private sub-contracting use. These federal funds were to be accounted for by representatives that were appointed by the people and ethically Tate felt he had a responsibility to do the peoples will. "You ok boss," asked Ray as Tate sat in the back seat, "Ray I feel like the last man standing," said Tate. "Don't worry about it boss, I got your back," replied Ray as he

screeched off in the SUV.

Tate Balling

Tate enjoyed his time home with his family and his son. Tate Jr. impressed him without end in his ability to learn about the statistics used in sports especially football. "How did you know the Miami Seahawks was the first professional football team to play seven games in the Orange Bowl son?" Tate asked.

Tate Jr. Looked perplexed and stuck his lip out, "It's called Wikipedia dad," he replied. Tate chuckled at his son's response while he relaxed on his leather couch. Tate received a call on his cell and stepped outside to take the call.

The call was from Jeremy, "Amp you and I have a meeting tomorrow morning with a major advertiser," he said.

"OK text me the info and I will meet you," Tate replied hanging up the phone with excitement in his voice.

***

Tate met with Jeremy the next morning in the lobby of the InterContinental Hotel in Metro Miami. As Tate approached Jeremy he noticed two well-dressed gentlemen with him. "Good Morning I'm Anthony Tate," said Tate as he shook hands with the gentlemen.

Jeremy interjected saying, "Tate these men are from Zephyrhills Hills, Florida and they represent the bottle water company." As they stood in the lobby people bustled by not noticing their discussion.

"They are interested in signing Haze to an advertising contract with an advancement of a hundred grand for an exclusive water marketing deal," said Jeremy.

Tate replied, "As manager I accept the proposal gentlemen."

Jeremy replied, "We can work out the details later."

"I will be in contact with your office regarding the paperwork," said Tate.

"If you will excuse us," said Jeremy to the men.

"Have a great stay in Miami," said Tate as he walked off with Jeremy. "How did you make that connect," Asked Tate?

Jeremy replied, "They called me out of the blue and said they got my number from Lisa."

"That's a big deal for us," said Tate. He slapped Jeremy on the back.

"We're moving up G," exclaimed Jeremy.

***

Later that night Tate held a party for the group at Club Rolex and most of the music entertainment celebs in Miami showed up for the event. Jeremy was posted up in the VIP lounge with two of the group members. Tate walked in VIP, "This is just the beginning boys, wait to the album release party," he replied.

Jeremy held up a glass of wine, "to Haze," he said and toasted the air.

Tate with some of the signing money from the bottle water deal leveraged it for a fifty thousand dollar loan and placed a down payment on a 2009

Maybach Landaulet convertible. Tate pulled up to his front lawn as Ray washed the SUV in the driveway.

"That's a beauty boss," Ray exclaimed!

"Yeah I bought it from a friend of the family for a pretty penny," said Tate.

"It's a nice pearl white," said Ray as he admired the car.

"Let's take it for a spin Ray," said Tate as he hopped in the back passenger seat and Ray took over at the wheel. Ray drove through the streets of Miami and on through the Tate's district with the top down in the back. People on the street looked in amazement as they waved to Tate roll by in his new ride.

"Ray hit the studio," said Tate from the back seat.

"Got you boss," Ray replied as he wheeled the car in the direction of the studio. Jeremy was outside smoking a black and mild with the members of Haze when Ray pulled up. "Like the Ride fellas?" said Ray from the back seat.

Jeremy was the first to speak, "Tight ride," he said with a big grin. The members of Haze were all admiring the rims and tires commenting on how nice they were.

"Everyone get in, we're off to CoCo's ," exclaimed Tate in a booming baritone voice. Everyone clamored into the car and Ray screeched off to the other side of town.

***

Coco's was a local strip club that was nationally known in the rap music industry for its various music video appearances depicting sexy

167

Miami women. Ray pulled up to the front of the club and everyone disembarked. "Boss I will be in the parking lot if you need me," replied Ray. Tate entered the club with the crew and they made a B-line for VIP as patrons checked out their entourage. The DJ began playing one of the group's singles as the club manager greeted them and escorted them to VIP.

Tate removed a knot of dollar bills from his front pocket, "Bring all your best girls," he said.

"Gentlemen the drinks are on the house," replied the manager.

A group of strippers made their way to the VIP section and were given a hundred dollars apiece to lap dance and entertain the Haze crew. Jeremy and Tate sat near a back table with two women on their laps.

"Wow did you do what I think you did," asked Jeremy as the fat bottomed girl gyrated on his lap making his nature rise.

"Don't worry about it," Tate replied. "I got checks cut for you guys in the car, you get your money now up front as opposed waiting for it to be dispersed by the company," said Tate. "No Strings attached."

"Cool with me," said Jeremy with a huge grin. "I spoke with Lisa and she said the company is looking to release the album in two weeks," said Jeremy.

"Do we get our advancements," asked Tate?

"I'm quite sure we have nothing to worry about," Jeremy replied.

A young stripper with a Bahamian accent sat on Tate's lap and gyrated to the beat of the music. She whispered in Tate's ear, "I know who you are."

"Who am I," Tate replied taking a sip from his glass.

"You're that commissioner guy," she said. "Not tonight baby," said Tate as he laughed and sipped his drink. "I'm the manager of the Hip Hop group Haze," Tate said toasting his glass with Jeremy's drink glass. Tate handed the club manager a stack of bills and said, "Kind sir can you get us some one's?"

***

An Engineer finished the mastering and mix of his work and forwarded the finished product to Lisa shilling's office. Lisa's secretary viewed the finished product and notified her boss, "Ms. Shilling the Haze project is all set and ready to go," the secretary replied. "Should I notify the manager and organize a listening party," she inquired.

"Fine," replied Lisa. "No wait," Lisa replied before the secretary could walk away with her orders. "Don't worry about notifying Commissioner Tate, I will be meeting with Jeremy later," she said. "I will let him know what's going on and what to expect," Lisa replied.

"Yes Ms. Shilling," said the secretary. "Well do you need anything else," asked the secretary. "I'm leaving for the day."

"No," replied Lisa, "See you tomorrow."

Tate sat in the back of his new ride on the way home from a long night. Ray blasted the music as they maneuvered through the dark streets of Miami. Tate's phone rang, "Yeah," he answered. He listened with intent as the smile on his face faded. "Ok Thanks," he said as he hung up his call.

"Everything good boss," Ray asked with a look of concern. Tate paused and sat in the thinking man's pose as he looked out the car window at the passing street lights. "Boss is everything alright," asked Ray again.

"Nothing I can't handle Ray" Said Tate.

Tate's Election Season

Tate's re-election bid was coming up in the next six months and he had planned to do more fundraising among friendly donators. He did a lot of his networking thru Terrence Kemp who was well known in the community and among community organizations. Tate met up with Terrence at Beale Street barber after getting his weekly haircut from Movay.

"I have some great ideas for your re-election Amp," said Terrence. "We're going to conduct business out of a nice new building I'm renting on the west side," Terrence stated.

"Sounds great," replied Tate. "I have a couple of organizations I plan to solicit for fund raising dinners also, and I plan to tour the district in my RV to solidify a presence in the district," said Tate.

The shop was crowded as usual with patrons walking in and out chatting about current world events. Tate and Terrence stood in one of the back barber booths where their conversation was private.

"I also have some donors interested in getting you re-elected, so expect to have many thousand dollar dinner plate swore-rays," Terrence said with a chuckle.

"Yeah I plan to run my campaign on my history of contributions I've made to the community in acquiring economic development grants," Tate commented.

"I think you should go after the bankers and mortgage industry for their shady business dealings," said Terrence.

"Are you nuts," Tate replied. "I will get buried running on that sort of ticket," he said. "Besides now is not the time for that," Tate responded.

"I disagree," said Terrence. "Government is not a good road to traverse in this season," Terrence stated.

"Well it's the route that ensembles my need," said Tate sternly.

Tate knew in politics getting elected was not that important but what happened after elections was. In American politics maintaining post-election ties with the elite political class of corporate funded think tanks, high powered law firms and prestigious universities are essential. These ties determine if you are able to work while between jobs or if you are able to run again in future political races. Your political life is determined by the way you walk the political tight rope so to speak. Tate knew Terrence had no concept of this practice as he looked in from the outside. This sort of things could not be taught by the books. Tate listened as Terrence debated passionately his point and why it was good for his ideal to be considered. Finally Tate responded, "Listen just stick to the logistics and I will run my campaign as I see fit!"

Terrence replied, "Fine."

Tate looked around the shop and continued, "Listen, set up the dinners for the next six month time span and volunteers will show up to help with the minor details."

"Ok," said Terrence. Turning to leave the shop Terrence said, "I will be in touch when I have things lined up."

As Terrence walked toward the shop exit Tate could only wonder if Terrence would be effective at accomplishing the task. Tate flopped down in the barber's chair with his head leaning back on the neck stand of the chair.

Movay walked over, "Yeah mon when you guys ever going to not go after each other's jugular," he said with a laugh.

Tate looked at him and shook his head, "my people," he replied still looking Movay in the eye.

"Don't worry we'll have something here at the shop mon," said Movay. "A fundraiser," he said in his Jamaican accent. Tate knew that the Caribbean base of his constituents could be rallied for support by Movay's gesture. The Haitians and Jamaicans in the district often take the backseat in the political process of the city.

"I appreciate your support," replied Tate.

***

Tate decided to take a ride through the district. Ray pulled the car up to the front of the shop as Tate bid the patrons in the shop good day. He told Ray to meet him a couple of blocks over and began to walk the sidewalk. As Tate walked the district he noticed the abandoned houses which were once homes to families. A group of men loitered around a rusted out barrel in one of the blighted lots. "What's up commissioner Amp," one man yelled. Tate waved a peace sign at the group as he strolled by on the sidewalk. Tate realized the importance of the community having jobs and people being able to work to provide for their families. Tate believed in achieving success and being comfortable but all that comes second in service to the community. Tate thought to himself it was ethically wrong to enrich oneself using public money pooled from the masses for personal self-indulgence. He did believe that capitalism built a great communal engine in Miami and supported the entrepreneurial spirit. Tate resolved to do the will of the people to the best of his ability.

Ray sat as the car idled on the next block. Tate crossed the street and slipped in the back seat as a young women waved to him from the front porch of a rundown duplex. "You ok," Ray asked.

"Yeah, it looks very bleak out there Ray," commented Tate.

"Yeah boss, we gotta get you re-elected so you can continue the good fight," said Ray.

"You're right," replied Tate. "I can't help but worry about Terrence," Commented Tate. "He seems to be headed down the wrong stretch," said Tate. "You know what I mean Ray," Tate asked as he sat forward in his seat.

"Well I tell you like this...a man has to walk his own path," responded Ray.

"I guess so Ray, I guess so," said Tate as his voice trailed off. He leaned back in his seat and the car jetted off into the noon sunlight. As they drove along Tate received a call on his cell and the caller ID displayed RON WIGGINS. "Mr. Wiggins," said Tate into the phone. "Yes I am preparing for the upcoming election and I could use all the support I can get," remarked Tate. "Great, I will call you and we can set up a location for the interview," Tate replied as he ended the call. Tate thought to himself a little free publicity would definitely be a boost for his campaign. He would have his secretary call and make arrangement for the interview to be conducted in the office. "Take me home Ray," said Tate. "I need to write up some plans while they are fresh on my mind," said Tate. "I'm quite sure Cherry could give me some ideas also with my campaign," said Tate aloud to himself.

***

Two men sat wrapped with white towels in a sauna at the Golf Pro Club their faces masked by the steam permeating the room. "I hear Tate is up for re-election," said the first man.

"Yeah," replied the second man.

"Let's make sure the message is clear, simple and plain," said the first man.

"Oh that goes without saying," said the second man as the two chuckled with mild glee.

An attendant opened the sauna's door, "anything more gentlemen," he asked.

"Just get us more towels son," quipped the first man. "And be quick about it

Betrayal

Haze's debut album was released at the beginning of the summer and two songs received regular radio play. The group was projected by the local radio station jocks to sell five hundred thousand copies within six months. Tate spoke with a few of the group members who had approached him concerning questions about their royalty statements.

Tate phoned Lisa at her office, "Lisa Shilling's Office," said the secretary. "Hey this is Amp I need to talk with Lisa," he said. "Ms. Shilling directed me to have you leave a message and she would return your call later commissioner," replied the secretary. "Fine," replied Tate with irritation in his voice. "She has my number, tell her it's about the royalty statements," he said before hanging up the call.

Tate viewed the royalty statements in question and had relayed to the group members that it largely delineated who was due what in regards to money generated. Tate had previously scolded Jeremy about not reading the contract terms before signing. Jeremy obviously had not passed on this vital piece of information to the other group members. Tate noticed that the company was getting considerable more points as compared with the joint membership of the group reflected on the statements. The members were clueless to what the actual meaning of the situation meant financially for them. Tate pitied them because these high school graduates were no matches for the Ivy league legal trained business savvy record label executive chiefs.

Tate was aware of the choices many non-scholastically inclined urban youth faced who grew up in poverty. Drugs, crime, sports and music were natural options for poor aspiring blacks. Many of Miami's most famous artist rose to dominance as a consequence of dope boys and make money makers whom financed the independent record movement. Tate knew first hand that many of those folks got life sentences, long prison bids and were buried in pine boxes six feet deep. Tate heard that in the 1980's and 1990's bricks of cocaine reigned through the port of Miami.

Tate took his role as manager of the group very seriously and he was now inspired to fully exercise his rights over the groups business deals. He was of the resolve to set up a meeting with Jeremy to discuss firming up his rights and duties as the manager of the budding Haze Empire.

***

Tate decided to attend a chamber of commerce meeting being held in metro Miami before contacting Jeremy. Chamber of commerce meetings were usually well attended by the elite and power brokers of Miami. The meeting was scheduled for noon and Tate decided to show up early expecting to leave before the meeting end. As he entered the posh lobby of the meeting room he ran into Lisa Shilling, "What a surprise," said Tate.

"Hello Commissioner," replied Lisa.

"Have you been dodging me," asked Tate.

"No sir actually I want to discuss a few contractual issues with you regarding Haze," she replied.

"Yeah I know," said Tate. "A couple of members were concerned about their royalty statements and points on the contract," said Tate.

"Not about that," replied Lisa. "To be frank with you Commissioner, you're out," said Lisa.

Looking perplexed Tate replied, "What do you mean out."

She placed a hand on his arm, "you don't have anything in writing with the group relating to the contract," Lisa replied. Tate stated adamantly, "I had an agreement with Jeremy." "We shook hands and as long as we both agreed no written statement is needed," remarked Tate.

"While that may be true the deal is entirely unenforceable," stated Lisa. "Sorry."

Tate replied, "I put a lot of energy and work into this project and am not going to just let that go."

Tate strode off and over his shoulder shot, "You have not heard the last of this."

Lisa stood with a smirk on her face as she watched Tate disappear out the door into the south Florida midday.

Tate now realized he should have recorded things on paper but his schedule was so hectic small details such as that often escaped him. He knew he should contact Jeremy and get him to contact Lisa as soon as possible. Tate knew performance in completing tasks were important in constituting a contract, and he had more than completed his share of tasks in making the group who they were in the business. Tate had to move quickly to stave off the attack the label was trying to pull off on his role with Haze. He first contacted his lawyer and set up a consultation to discuss the issue of contract law. He then phoned the group members and scheduled a mandatory meeting at the studio later that night. Finally he dialed Jeremy's number; it rang and rang going directly to voice mail on the fourth ring.

***

It was late in the hour that Tate assembled the meeting with Haze and all were in attendance with the exception of Jeremy. "As you may have heard the label is trying to squeeze me out of the contract with the group," said Tate. Rumblings instantly echoed through the group members as Tate paused for reactions. "I have continuously tried to contact Jeremy to no avail," said Tate. "I was unable to properly address your concerns about the contract but I will continue to push the issue," Tate stated. "I will retain a lawyer if need be and I do plan to fight the label regarding this issue," said Tate. The group members applauded with delight. The meeting ended on a positive note and Tate exited the studio with the group members. Tate stood outside along the walk way and lit a cigar as he watched the last member of Haze leave the premises.

"Amp," said Jeremy as he walked up from the back side of the studio building.

Tate turned in the direction of Jeremy and knocked the ashes from his cigar as Jeremy approached him.

"Where you been Jeremy?" asked Tate sarcastically.

"Hey man, I heard what's going down with Lisa and I had nothing to do with it," stated Jeremy. "They see it as a way of cutting cost to enlarge their profit margin," said Jeremy. "I know we have a deal and I will honor it," said Jeremy as he took a cigarette cartoon from his pocket tapped it against his thigh removed a cigarette and lit it. Tate finished one last puff of his cigar outed it and walked away. "Amp," yelled Jeremy, "where you going man?" Tate continued on not responding to Jeremy's inquiry. "I got your back man, I got you back!" Jeremy's words echoed through the empty streets as the night air blew in from the beach.

***

Trans – Sexual & Drugs

Tate helped many friends while working in leadership for the city. One such friend relocated from out of state and Tate assisted him in attaining employment. Shay Jackson was Tate's friend from childhood. Shay had grown up in an all-female household and possessed feminine traits as a young male growing up. It was later revealed that Shay was a homosexual when he went off to college and began living on his own in Atlanta. Tate entered Mercy hospital located in the heart of Liberty City, "Is there a Shay Jackson checked in here?" he asked the front desk attendant. "Room 112," the attendant responded without looking up. Tate made his way to the room pushing the door open he saw his friend in the bed.

"Amp, I didn't think you would come see about me," said Shay.

"Man what happened?" Tate inquired as he pulled a chair up and sat by the bed.

"I was on my way home after performing at the downtown cabaret and I stopped in at a local bar for a quick drink," said Shay. "As I was there a guy bought me a drink and we began talking," Shay paused for a second then continued. "Basically he tried to get fresh with me discovered I was a man and shot me," said Shay with tears welling in his eyes.

Tate doubled over roaring with laughter. "So what you mean is, you tried to pick up a man in drag and he shot you when you didn't have a clit," said Tate wiping his eyes.

193

"Whatever Amp," replied Shay smacking his lips.

"I told you a million times you can't come down here with that sort a deception," said Tate with a chuckle. "You got to be yourself," Tate stated. "You're lucky you weren't killed out there," said Tate in a serious tone. "What were you doing, out looking for a quick hit?" Tate inquired.

"No I was just having some fun like anyone else," said Shay.

"You're definitely not going to meet someone to settle with doing those night flyer methods," replied Tate.

"Well I have a couple of friends that express an interest in you Amp," replied Shay.

"You know I don't roll like that," said Tate with a look of disgust on his face. "Yeah well I have a couple of friends down at the cabaret who said

otherwise about your boys in blue," said Shay.

"Especially that holier than thou chief," said

Shay as he sat up in his bed and winced in pain from

his gunshot wound. Tate stared at Shay in disbelief

as to the revelation he just heard. "What?" Shay

asked. "You heard me," said Shay. "The boys in blue

hold these poker games a couple of times a month

and sometimes they invite performers from the

cabaret to do shows," stated Shay. "At one of the

shows the Chief was there," said Shay in a matter of

fact tone. A huge grin came over Tate's face.

"Yeah, can your friends get a hold of some

pictures?" inquired Tate.

"I don't know about that but I will let you

know," said Shay. Tate took out his wallet and

counted out four hundred fifty dollars and handed it to Shay.

"Make sure you friends know that I am serious about getting those pictures," he said. Shay snatched the money and tucked it under his pillow.

"The message is clearer than a bell," said Shay. "They're letting me out soon, can I get a ride home with you," asked Shay looking around for his clothes.

"As long as you're not in drag no problem," stated Tate.

"The doctor said I only have a flesh wound but it hurts like hell," said Shay.

The doctor entered with a nurse, "Mr. Jackson we're releasing you in your own reconnaissance," she said.

"See ya, doc," exclaimed Shay as Tate helped him into a nearby wheel chair.

"Oh here's a prescription for pain killers for any discomfort you may experience," said the nurse as he handed Shay the paper.

Shay snatched the paper and replied, "Thanks but I have my own remedy." Tate briskly wheeled Shay out the door toward the hospital exit. As they maneuvered toward the curb Ray pulled up in the car cutting off a waiting Taxi and opened the back passenger door. "Nice wheels," exclaimed Shay as Tate helped him into the back seat. Ray hit the gas and the Taxi driver angrily blew his horn as the car sped off onto the freeway headed out of the parking lot. "I need another favor Amp before you drop me home," said Shay.

"What's that," said Tate as he reclined in the back seat.

"I need some blow and weed," replied Shay. "Take me over by the poke and bean to holla at my main home boy," said Shay.

Tate looked at Shay in disbelief, "Are you out of your mind!" he exclaimed.

"I'm not taking you to no dope hole," stated Tate shaking his head from side to side. "The only reason I look out for you the way I do is because I consider myself to be real," Tate replied. "I look out for my friends, family and people I care about," said Tate. "I Keeps it real," stated Tate. "You are definitely pushing the envelope but here is what I can do for you," said Tate. "Ray drop our guest off on 54th Street," stated Tate. "You go make your pick up and do what you gotta do." said Tate. "Give me a call when you are ready to go home." Ray stopped the car on the corner of 54ᵗʰ and Shay got out. The car sped off as Ray view shay's image in the rearview mirror crossing the busy street. "Who's the pansy?" Ray asked.

"An old neighborhood friend from back in the day," remarked Tate.

Tate believed it was important to keep his real friends around, and utilize what they brought to the friendship in order to enhance his own life. He was fortunate Shay's network of contacts could possibly help him professionally in getting leverage on his enemy. Tate knew his relationship with Shay could be viewed as questionable because of Shay's sexuality. However, Tate was never the kind of person to let another's opinion of him affect his actions.

"What you wanna do boss?" Ray asked as they turned off 54ᵗʰ Street onto the next block.

Tate paused for a moment and then replied, "Drop me off home Ray and park the car." "Take the SUV come back pick Shay up and take him where he wants to go," said Tate.

"No problem boss," replied Ray.

Ray was deep in thought about the possibility of getting one up on the chief who was definitely a thorn in his administration. It would be a media storm if it was leaked that off duty police officers hire gay performers for their monthly poker games. Especially damaging would the chief's involvement in attending such events. Tate would ensure that Shay would be well taken care of until he could get more information regarding the subversive operations of the boys in blue.

Ray drove over to the dope spot by 54th street and waited for Shay to call for a lift home as instructed by Tate. Ray's phone rang and he answered it, "Hey Boss, yeah I'm in place." Ray ended the call and waited. He soon saw Shay as he walked out into the street. Ray pulled up along the side of the curb, "Hop in," he said to Shay. "I see Amp has really come of age," Shay said as he made himself comfortable in the back seat. "You're association with him can really be used to compromise his integrity," commented Ray. "I hope your friendship is as true as his," said Ray. "Because you and I certainly will have a conversation if otherwise," Ray said as he patted the side of his waist band. Shay cringed in the back seat of the SUV.

***

Jeremy Unveiled

Tate walked in Terrence's office at the community center while Terrence was having lunch at his desk.

"Would you care for lunch Amp?" asked Terrence.

Tate replied, "naw my stomach has been quizzy lately," he rubbed his belly.

"I heard some dirt about one of the cats you do business with Amp," said Terrence as he ate his lunch.

"Yeah who's that?" asked Tate as he watched Terrence wipe his mouth before he replied.

"Jeremy," he said.

"I didn't know you knew Jeremy personally," Tate replied in astonishment.

"I know him from the neighborhood," said Terrence. "He always had a hustle going on and he was into the music thing early on," Terrence stated. "That guy's a snake, snitch and a low life," said Terrence as he munched his sandwich.

Tate view of Jeremy was not of his life on the streets but of how he presented himself to people in his company. He knew little of Jeremy's street reputation but had noticed a change in Jeremy's behavior lately.

Terrence polished off his lunch and said, "I heard he got busted on the dock with a couple of keys of coke."

Tate folded his arms and continued to stand in front of Terrence's desk. "Yeah," he replied.

Terrence took a napkin and wiped his hands, "he will sing like a bird to the feds to get out of his predicament," said Terrence with a laugh.

Tate watched Terrence as he cleaned the area on the desk where he had lunch.

"Talk in the streets is Jeremy is a government informant and is incredibly manipulative in getting himself out of tight situations," said Terrence.

Tate knew he needed to find out more details on what was going on with Jeremy's situation. Jeremy seemed to be a formidable Machiavellian force when navigating in business in Tate's assessment.

"Do you think you can find out more information and get back to me?" asked Tate.

"I will keep my ear to the ground and let you know of anything I hear about," replied Terrence.

Tate began to have second thoughts on how the contract issue with the music label went down. Maybe Jeremy had a hand in what happened and knew what Lisa's intentions were. After all they did seem to have more than a professional relationship Tate speculated. "I will talk to you later," said Tate as he left the office and headed for the community center parking lot. He was unsure which direction to go but he knew it was not a time for procrastination.

***

Two men in suits approached Jeremy as he walked out of Beale Street barbershop, "Mr. Coons can we have a word," said one of the men.

"Why you guys sweating me," replied Jeremy. "I was clear about this kind of thing early on," he remarked as he looked over his shoulder.

"We were told you had a package to pass along," said one of the suits.

"Let's walk," replied Jeremy. Jeremy pulled a folded envelop from his pocket and handed it to one of the men. "This contains contact information of a witness that can confirm your bribery suspicions of the commissioner," said Jeremy. "He has just lost his business contacts with one of the major music labels," stated Jeremy as he walked at a brisk pace. "Yo he will really be out to beat the brush to see what falls out," said Jeremy.

"Great thanks for your cooperation," said one of the suited men.

They both immediately crossed the street and got in a grey Crown Victoria vehicle with dark tints. Jeremy continued up the street not noticing Movay on the sidewalk. Movay took one last pull from his black-n-mild cigar stamped it out and walked back inside the barbershop.

***

Tate entered Beale Street for his regular trim and haircut.

"What's good?" he said as he greeted Movay and gave up a fist bump. Tate sat down in the barber's chair and Movay placed the apron around his neck to begin his work.

"Have you seen Jeremy around?" Inquired Tate.

"He twas here earlier mon," replied Movay with his heavy Jamaican accent. "I saw him outside the shop with what looked like cops." Those words felt like hot daggers to Tate as they rolled off Movay's tongue.

Tate turned in his chair to look Movay in the face. "Cops?" he said.

"yeah," said Movay. "They look like the Feds you know with the dark sunglasses and Brooks Brothers suites mon," said Movay.

"They spoke to him for a while and then took off in a Crown Vic and Jeremy walked up the bloc," stated Movay. "I heard bout Jeremy mon, he a bad boy," said Movay shaking his head. "Mon have no heart, no loyalty," commented Movay.

Tate leaned back in the chair, "I wish I would've known this before," said Tate.

"You know he and a buddy of mine got busted with a key down at the port last week," said Movay. "My buddy is locked down about to get deported and Jeremy still out walking around mon," stated Movay as he waved the clippers around in the air.

"Yeah those are all the trappings of a rat," said Tate under his breath.

***

Jeremy stepped off the elevator entering Lisa's office, "What's up gorgeous you ready for our dinner date?" He inquired.

"In a minute, just need to finish some paperwork." Lisa replied.

"You know I didn't mean for you to hit Amp that hard with the news," commented Jeremy. "After all we did shake hands on the deal and he was a great boost for us in getting local recognition in the music scene," said Jeremy. "Well pay him from your pocket," Lisa replied in a terse tone. "Let's not be ridiculous," said Jeremy as he flopped on a nearby sofa.

"The commissioner's a big boy," said Lisa. "I'm quite sure he will forget about his short venture in the Hip Hop business after a couple of weeks."

Jeremy shifted in his seat, "Maybe." He replied. "Amp is a real sore loser and what's worse the man is like an elephant he forgets nothing," Jeremy stated. "Black politicians are like royalty in this community, he is considered King or more of an overlord in his district."

Lisa looked up from what she was doing, "well he will not have to worry about being king in the area of artist management."

Jeremy ignored Lisa's remark and continued, "All I'm saying is you should try to cut the man a deal before making such a powerful enemy."

Lisa finished up her work and grabbed her portfolio, "let's go."

Ray flicked his cigarette butt to the ground as he folded his umbrella to get back inside the car out of the rain. Tate sat in the backseat looking out the window as the water poured from the sky like a water fall. "It's raining cats and dogs boss," said Ray.

"Yeah speaking of dogs," said Tate as he watched Jeremy and Lisa exit the front entrance of the Light Star Entertainment building. Ray turned the wipers off on the car to get a better view of the couple.

"What do you want to do, should I follow them Boss," asked Ray.

"Forget about it Ray," said Tate as he reclined in the back seat. "Every dog is do his day and a bitch

211

will get kicked," said Tate. They both watched the rear tail lights of the car back out and turn out of the parking lot onto the street. The rain continued to pour down, Ray reached over and turned the wipers on again as the car disappeared up the street.

The Edge

Tate entered Central Pentecostal which was a main prominent black church in his Overtown district. He sat down in the back row of the bleachers and instantly bowed his head in the still silence to pray. While Tate had come from a religious upbringing he was distanced by the obsession in making it in the world. Being successful epitomized the American dream of cars, houses, women, power and tons of money. Tate's family lineage included former deacons, church mothers and even church pastors dating back to the Jim Crow era in the south. Tate reminisced when as a child seeing the church ladies with their decorative hats. The ushers dressed with their white gloves and outfits serving as the church's security forces. The sweat drenched pastors preaching in the pulpit whaling about god's good glory to the masses of the congregation.

Tate thought to himself as a youth he cared little about spirituality and truly wanted to avoid the damnation of Hell at all costs. Now as an adult his mortality was inevitable and he absolutely saw the need to have his spirit right with god. Tate's father had an adage he was often fond of saying, "if you lay down with dogs you will often wind up with fleas." Tate in all his experiences could finally realize the wisdom of his father's words. In analyzing his own troubles he was slowly being pulled down with those he wished to not become.

He despised the system which he had been cast into for its belittling categorization of people. Tate believed that he could help the masses of people he represent in his district. With his education, experience and insights he believed he could make the circumstances of his people better. His father would often extol being a success and making it in the American system. What's the true definition of success Tate often contemplated? Was it success to be a dominate player at what you do? Or was it to do good by those in your realm of influence and be appreciated for your deeds. Tate initially began his career in service to the people and community which led to his current tumultuous quandary. He was essentially caught in a chess match in that he unknowingly maneuvered in a checkers mode mentality. He was not just playing to win the game; he was playing to survive for life.

As Tate sat in contemplation with his head bowed he felt a hand on his shoulder and he looked up. The church pastor a slightly graying elderly gentleman stood over him with a solemn expression on his face, "son I will pray for you." He said. Tate knew in his heart that doing the right thing was more important than anything else. He arose and with a mighty stride, exited the church with a new conviction.

***

Tate made it back to his office and began arranging meet times with Commissioner Sancho and his partner Magoya. They would meet at the Golf Pro club and there Jeremy would be introduced to the pair. Tate phoned Jeremy and got no answer so he left a message on his answering service. Tate decided to head over to the studio to meet with the group. As

Tate pulled up to the studio he spotted Jeremy walking out.

"Jeremy you're not returning calls or something?" he asked as he walked up to Jeremy on the street side walk. "Man I just left you a message," said Tate.

Jeremy responded nervously, "Tate, yo man I've been meaning to get back at you." Jeremy looked around and said, "I have so much going on with me you know."

Take replied, "Listen I want you to attend this meeting with me later."

Pulling Jeremy aside Tate continued, "I have some very important people for you to meet that could be perspective investors for you man." Tate knew anything that had to do with money would elicit a positive response from Jeremy.

217

Jeremy enthusiastically replied, "Just let me know when and where man."

Jeremy clapped his hands together and rubbed them furiously in anticipation of new money. Listen man he turned to Tate and said, "I'm working to fix that thing with Lisa."

Tate replied, "You better."

Jeremy shrugged, "Lisa's about the bottom line and money man."

Tate responded, "I wouldn't expect less from a business minded women like her." Tate knew how executives operated all too well and respected the game. "I respect the game but I got no luv for it," replied Tate.

"Well I'm definitely learning and like I told you before I got you," said Jeremy.

Tate turned his back and said, "See you at the meeting Jeremy."

As Ray drove Tate reclined in the back seat, he pondered about his work schedule and what needed to be discussed at the meeting. "Boss I think we are being tailed," said Ray from the front seat. Tate replied, "You sure."

Ray glanced in the rearview mirror. "It looks like an unmarked government car," he said.

"Don't worry about it Ray," said Tate.

"We're not breaking any rules." Ray continued to drive and the car followed their every turn. Ray pulled up at the country club and was greeted by Raul's assistant in the drive way. He directed Ray to park in a special parking area and Tate was told where the meeting was to take place. Tate texted Jeremy the location details as he walked in the club house's main lobby area. Tate entered a corner room where Raul sat at the bar watching the football game.

"Amp good to see you," pepped Raul. Tate soon saw Chris in the back of the room chatting intently on the phone. Tate walked over and pumped Raul's outstretched hand.

"My man will be here in a second," he said to Raul settling in a nearby chair. "This kid Jeremy has a great business sense and is generating good money on the national music scene," said Tate.

"Yeah Ok," replied Raul as he knocked back a cocktail and continued to watch the game.

Raul's assistant soon entered the room followed by Jeremy, "This place is awesome," said Jeremy. Chris strolled over to the bar as he ended his conversation on his cell phone.

"Jeremy these are the gentlemen I was telling you about," said Tate.

"You're in the music business, huh," said Chris.

"Yeah," replied Jeremy.

"This is what we want you to do," said Raul. "The videos you do will be shot at specific locations designated by me on properties owned by my buddy here." Raul took a sip from a shot glass and looked around the room. "Your permit will be covered and the million dollar deposit for the insurance will come to me." Jeremy looked at Tate and Tate shrugged his shoulders.

"What am I getting out the deal," asked Jeremy.

"No problems with city government and some new friends," replied Raul.

Tate walked to the bar and placed an order for rum with tonic. "Have a drink." Raul said to Jeremy. "It's on me." He motioned for a waitress.

"Touch down," exclaimed Chris as he clapped his hands and grinned broadly as the game ended on the television.

***

Tate walked into his office and was immediately notified by his secretary there was a visitor waiting to meet with him. Ron Wiggins without a scheduled meeting had showed up unannounced to meet with Tate. Tate walked into his office and motioned for the secretary to send Ron in.

"Hello commissioner sorry for the unexpected intrusion," Ron commented.

Tate shook Ron's hand and responded, "No problem Ron."

Tate settled into his office chair and asked, "What can I do you for Ron?"

Ron looked over his shoulder and took out a note pad, "I've heard from a source that you're being investigated for bribery."

Tate leaned back in his chair, "If I am I'm the last to know," chuckled Tate.

"Seriously commissioner," Ron responded.

Tate leaned forward in his chair and looked Ron in the eyes. "Ron I'm unaware of any investigation, especially one against me," said Tate. Ron looked perplexed and began to fidget with the pages of the note pad. "I do appreciate you giving me the heads up if I am to be investigated," replied Tate.

"Well I thought I would try to corroborate what was told to me with you, sorry for any inconvenience," said Ron.

"No inconvenience," replied Tate. "As a matter of fact I want you to contact me about anything you have questions about," commented Tate.

"Thank you commissioner," said Ron as he exited the office.

Tate immediately called his attorney and was advised to take care of any loose ends in all his affairs. Tate was unsure what to make of Ron Wiggins and he certainly had no trust for reporters. Ron seemed to him as an even keeled person but for a story and profit some reporters will sell their souls thought Tate as he pondered his predicament. Tate thought of making a call to the chief however he knew his relationship with him was quite contentious at best. He thought maybe he could reach out through Commissioner Sancho but he did not want Raul knowledgeable of his business matters. Tate decided to use an intermediary to beat the bush and find out about the status of any investigation taking place against him. He phoned Ray and told Ray to meet him outside his office. Ray wheeled the car up to the front building exit and Tate hoped in back.

"Ray I need you to utilized your resources and find out if there is an investigation going on against me, "said Tate.

Ray looked in the rear view, "No problem boss," he replied. "You can count on me," replied Ray.

***

Jeremy stepped off the elevator and entered Lisa's office as she sat reviewing new contracts of signed artists.

"Jeremy it seems we have a problem," she said as she glanced up from her stack of papers. "I received a call from the commissioner's attorney and it seems your oral agreement with him may have validity," she stated as she shuffled some papers. "They plan to sue if we don't negotiate a deal with them."

Jeremy flopped in a nearby chair, "I say cut him a deal," he replied.

Lisa replied, "Yeah you may need to have a chat with him and see what he wants."

Jeremy said, "I warned you not to play around with Amp."

"We will see what he wants and low ball him anyway," said Lisa as she continued to leaf through the contracts on her desk.

"You're one shrewd business woman," said Jeremy, "That's what makes you sexy!"

***

Ray pulled the car up to the front building of the studio and Tate hopped out headed to the main office. He entered the studio as some of the members were in the booth finishing up remixes on a couple of tracks they made. "Have you seen Jeremy?" He asked one of the engineers. The guy with speakers on his head shook his head in the negative. One of the members of the group Haze walked out of the booth.

"Amp if you're looking for Jeremy we haven't seen him all week," the group member replied.

"Yeah it seems harder and harder to catch up with that guy now-a-days," said Tate. "Listen man let the other members know that I need them to sign this management contract," said Tate.

"Hold on a minute," said the group member. He went into the booth cleared it out and corralled the other Haze members from downstairs. "We will all sign with you Amp," said the initial Haze member and Tate slapped the paper down on a nearby stand for them to sign. Tate walked out the studio pleased that he had the contracts signed by most of the members. Jeremy was the only member that he needed a signature from thought Tate as he got into his awaiting car.

"You look like you just won a million dollars," said Ray.

"I hope so," Tate replied. "All I need to do now is catch up with Jeremy and I truly will be in the money," said Tate.

"Don't worry about a thing boss," said Ray. "I will track him down for you and you don't have to worry about no problems from him again," said Ray.

***

Tate took a drive through his district and was appalled by the number of distressed properties within the neighborhoods. The fall of the real estate market caused detrimental ripple effects throughout the entire community. Tate remembered a time in his district when small businesses thrived in the community. Specifically black business owners were active residents in the community with defined leadership roles in the neighborhoods. Places such as the Lyric Theater and the Longshoremen's Union office assisted in the economic development of the community. Ray pulled the car up at a local corner store to run in for some smokes. Tate exited the vehicle and surveyed the area as an elderly gentleman came out of the store complaining loudly.

"Commissioner Tate, how are you?" The man said marveling at Tate's car.

"Fine just out visiting the community," Tate replied.

"Well you need to get some loans for some of us black entrepreneurs," said the elderly man.

"All the stores here are owned by the dag-blasted Indians, Koreans and the Arabians," remarked the elderly gentlemen. "Their customer service is horrible and they try to cheat you out of all your money," he went on. "They can't count," replied the old man. Ray walked out of the store and noticed the man talking loudly to Tate waving his hands.

"Boss the guy bothering you?" he inquired as he neared the two.

"Everything is fine Ray just having a friendly chat," replied Tate. Tate took a card from his pocket and pressed it in the old man's hand. "Give my office a call and we could try to assist you in this issue," Tate remarked as he got into his car. Tate enjoyed his visits to the community but the bombardment of constituents desiring this favor and that service could be overwhelming. Tate sat back in his seat and pondered what he could do to better serve the average everyday constituent. Serving the small business owner was an entire separate issue in assessing community needs. As a public service representative, family man and an entrepreneur in his

231

own right Tate knew he had to be well adept at managing stress. His personal issues would have to take a back seat to his duties of community service. "Ray take me by the community center," said Tate. "I have a few things to discuss with Terrence," he said.

"Sure thing boss," responded Ray.

Favors

Ron Wiggins sat at his office desk in the Miami News building and reviewed a press release on his email for an upcoming story he was contemplated covering. The office was not cluttered with writers and reporters as in normal times. Many press personal have been laid off or released due to the decline in newspaper print sales and the rise in internet viewer subscriptions.

"Ron I hear you're circling over the Commissioner Tate story," said one of his co-workers.

"You better be careful I hear he's a tricky son-of-a bitch," said Ron's co-worker. Ron ignored the comment and continued looking at his desk monitor checking his emails. His phone rings at his desk and he answers it, "Yeah this is Ron," he said into the receiver. "Great be there in ten," he said and hung up the phone. "I guess I'll see just how tricky he is," Ron commented to his co-worker as he bounded out the door.

***

Inside Dora's Rib Emporium the waitresses hurried about taking orders and serving rib combo sandwiches to the patrons. Tate sat in a corner booth facing the door, "Are you ordering now commissioner?" asked a young waitress with pimples on her face.

"Sure darling bring me a double order of the rib combo and a pitcher of Ice tea," said Tate.

Just as the waitress was about to leave with the order Ron walked in the door.

"Ron," yelled Tate motioning him over to the booth.

"Anything for you sir," inquired the waitress.

"I got him sweet heart," said Tate to the waitress.

"Thanks commissioner," replied Ron as he slid into the booth.

"Have you ever tried Dora's chicken?" Tate asked.

"No never," replied Ron.

"There're the best in town," replied Tate. "Ron I want to be frank with you," said Tate. "I believe I'm being targeted as some type of vendetta against my character," Tate paused as the waitress placed the food on the table. "I think you're capable of doing some digging and getting to the bottom of this thing," Tate said as he chomped on a wing.

"Look at it this way Ron," Tate continued. "You find something; you get to print the story," said Tate as he gnawed at the bone.

Ron adjusted hi spectacles, "Well I was not expecting this but you have any leads?" He asked.

Tate put down his food and looked Ron in the eyes. "Why don't you start with the Chief of police," he said.

Ron took out his note pad and jotted a few lines on the paper.

"In the meantime dig in," said Tate as he motioned for Ron to eat.

***

Tate arrived at Overtown's community center during the early morning hours and the offices were nearly empty. He walked into Terrence's office as Terrence leafed through the morning's paper. "Amp what're you doing up so early," Terrence remarked jokingly.

"Good Morning I wanted to talk with you about Raul and his crony Chris," Tate remarked.

"Yeah," responded Terrence as he folded the newspaper and tucked it up under his desk.

"I've evidence that Magoya Enterprises has been double billing the Pharmaceutical Park Project," remarked Tate. "They're using my district's money as a slush fund to construct their own personal playgrounds," Tate exclaimed. "The district residents are not interested in a casino or those high end bourgeois stores."

Terrene leaned back in his chair, "Amp don't you think you're overreacting a bit," he said. "Your district will more than likely benefit from the construction jobs and the money this will generate," said Terrence.

"You seem to be straddling the fence on this thing Terrence," said Tate. "I Know team Magoya has probably promised you something more than the little rental space he's given you but he is full it," remarked Tate.

Terrence folded his arms, "Yeah he has promised a lot of things Amp but the community needs change."

Tate paced the office floor, "this type of development is not economic freedom it's economic slavery." He exclaimed, "It's the engendering of a system designed to control the populous."

Terrence scratched his head in disbelief, "I think you are way off," he replied. "What do you want me to do," he asked.

Tate walked over to the window in Terrence's office, "I need you to watch my back," he said. "I'm not sure that they realize that I'm aware of what they are doing," said Tate. "This conversation never happened and if I hear of it I know exactly where it came from," Tate stated.

"I got you loud and clear," said Terrence.

The community center was abuzz with people coming in for their work shift and local community youth participating in job training seminars conducted in various conference rooms throughout the complex. The community center is representative of what the interests and needs of the residents in the district thought Tate as he walked out of the building.

***

Tate decided to promulgate this culture in all future endeavors. Tate caught up with his friend

Shay Jackson just as he was leaving Beale Street barbershop.

"Shay I've been meaning to catch up with you about a problem I have," said Tate.

"What's up Amp," replied Shay.

Tate pulled Shay to the side and asked, "What days do the cops hang out at the cabaret?"

Shay pondered for a moment then replied, "Generally it's on a Friday about once a week is routine." Shay had just gotten a fresh tape from the barber and he brushed the hair from his shirt as he chatted with Tate. "They come in buy rounds and get toasted," said Shay.

"When do you and your friends have major events in the club," inquired Tate.

"It's mostly a random thing outside of holidays, why?" replied Shay.

Tate leaned closer to Shay and said, "I want you hand your friends to advertise you're having this huge event at the club," said Tate.

"You can call it whatever you want but try to get as many cops there as you can." Shay smacking his lips replied, "Honey that type of thing takes money."

Tate reached in his pocket and pulled out a wad of cash. He peeled off two C notes and said, "Make it happen."

Shay snatched the money from his hand and said, "When do you want this to take place?"

Tate paused for a moment and replied, "I will call you with the details."

Tate stood outside the barbershop after his chat with Shay was over and smoked a fat hand rolled cigar. He knew with a little cash as a down payment

Shay would put all the things needed for his plan in motion. As Tate stood and smoked he visualized the details if his plan Ray walked up, "Can I bum a smoke from ya boss?" He asked.

Tate took two cigars from his inside sport jacket pocket and handed them to Ray. "One for now and one for later," he remarked. Ray pocketed one and held the other up gesturing for a lite from Tate.

"Ray I need you to do a couple of tasks for me, "Tate stated as he extended a lite for him. "Nothing illegal of course," said Tate. Ray took in a couple of quick pulls to ensure the cigar was lit. He then took one long drag filled his lungs with smoke and blew it out with a thunderous cough. "Can't handle the real thing, huh," said Tate with a heavy pat on Ray's back.

Ray cleared his voice and remarked, "Boss I will not do anything you ask me not to do."

Ray Sutter Unleashed

Ray stood in the mirror and dressed for work as was his normal routine on mornings before going on the job. He wore a loose fitting black Guayabera shirt and black Khaki pants with black hard bottomed shoes. He made sure to dab himself with good fragranced cologne as he liked to be complemented on the way he smell. He removed his switch blade from atop his dresser and tucked it in his pocked. He moved about his room and reached under his mattress for his snub nose .22 with the taped black handle. Ray was well prepared for any violence that may come his way and he was not shy about drawing blood.

Ray was on his way out the door when he was stopped by his mother. "Ray do you want breakfast," she asked. "No Ma," he replied as he walked out the door shutting it behind him.   The car was parked in the back of the house Tate allowed Ray to take it home so he could be on call when he needed him. Ray took the cover off the car placed it in the trunk and wiped it down with a cotton towel.

Ray anticipated an active day today and he checked his cell for messages, as he seated himself in the car. Ray drove over to the studio and waited across the street for the possibility of Jeremy showing up. Jeremy showed up at the studio an hour later and lingered outside awhile as he smoked a cigarette. Ray got out of the car took a hammer out of the trunk and put it in the small of his back up under his shirt.

He walked across the street towards Jeremy, "Morning Mr. Coons can I have a word," said Ray.

"What's up?" Jeremy replied.

Ray removed the hammer from his back and struck Jeremy in the top of the head. Jeremy instantly swallowed his cigarette and buckled at the knees as Ray swung him into the back alley of the building. His back hitting the wall Jeremy slid down and plopped on his rear with a thud.

Ray took a piece of paper from his back pocket unfolded it and asked, "Do you know what this is Mr. Coons?" Jeremy dazed tried to focus his eyes on the paper in front of him but was unable to speak. "Do you know what this is?" asked Ray again.

"A blank piece of paper," Jeremy finally remarked.

"No this is a contract that needs to be signed for Amp," said Ray. Ray handed Jeremy a pen, "Will you do the honors?" asked Ray. Jeremy sniffled, took the pen from Ray's hand and signed. "See now that wasn't so hard," said Ray as he walked out of the alley.

***

Ray got in the car and scrolled through his cell phone for messages he may have missed while he was out. He dialed up Ron Wiggins at his office, "Hello Ron this Ray," he said into the receiver. "Yeah Commissioner Tate's driver," He said. "Listen I would like to meet up with you and discuss some concerns of the commissioner," said Ray. "I'm over at the Cabaret on 72nd," said Ray. "Great ten minutes," said Ray as he ended the call. Ray drove to the Cabaret's parking area and checked his phone again before he went in. Ron walked through the doors of the Cabaret ten minutes later and walked over to a corner table where Ray sat. "How's it going Ray," said Ron as he took a seat. Ray motioned to the waitress and requested two doubles of patron.

"Ron I'm going to be straight with you," said Ray. "My offer is to give you a gift wrapped story of government employees violating the ethics of their duties and all you have to do is report it," said Ray.

"That sounds too good to be true," replied Ron.

Ray knocked back a shot of the patron and wiped his mouth. "Do you want the details or not," he asked. Ray motioned for Ron to drink the shot.

"What's the catch and why me?" Ron asked.

"Listen it's rumored the cops have wild parties in this very bar with cross dressers," said Ray. "I even hear the chief involved with the festivities and it's possible they do it while still on duty," Ray commented.

"Has this story been corroborated?" Ron asked.

"Ain't my job to corroborate," said Ray. Ray took a cigarette from his shirt pocket lit it and took a long pull. "I hear they get together on Friday nights," said Ray in between pulls. "Hell you're the reporter that's why I brought this to you," said Ray. "Most reporters get sold stories this is free with no strings attached," remarked Ray.

"So you're saying the cops' party with transvestites and the Chief condones of this activity," asked Ron.

"I'm saying the chief has partied with them but don't quote me on that or use me as a source, "commented Ray.

"All I'm saying is you can check it out or somebody else will probably run the story," said Ray. "I heard this from a credible source that was there when it happened," said Ray.

"Well I guess it won't hurt if I try to corroborate the story," said Ron aloud to himself. He reached over and took a shot of the patron. Ray and Ron continued to sit at the table and exchange rounds of patron as they chatted about the state of things in the city.

"What do you know about this supposed investigation of the commissioner," asked Ray.

"Well it's not really an investigation it's more of a fact finding to obtain evidence," said Ron.

Ron was inebriated after going shot for shot with Ray and it was not even twelve O'clock noon yet. "You mean to say they are trying to dig up something on the commissioner," Ray inquired.

"Well they have been tailing him for a couple of weeks," said Ron with slightly slurred words.

"If they find anything they will probably indict him," he said. Ray was not drunk due to his high tolerance for liquor. As they continued to drink Ron put his head on the table and eventually passed out. Ray walked over to the bar and waited for the bartender to pay the tab for the numerous drinks ordered. As the bartender took care of a patron Ray overheard two plain clothed cops talking about a stakeout they were conducting. One cop talked of shadowing a commissioner whenever he came in or out city hall. They also talked of setting up future stakeouts and questioning any person observed while monitoring this individual. Ray knew the two were referring to Commissioner Tate and made a mental note of the two individuals. Tate left Ron at the table still in a comatose state as he walked out he chuckled to himself and hit the door.

***

Ray sat in the car as he contemplated the new found information he learned of and he sent a text to Tate. His day was half over and he felt he'd completed twenty four hours of back breaking laborious work.

Tate sat in his office and browsed over emailed communications he received throughout the day. His cell phone vibrated violently atop of his desk almost toppling to the floor as Tate caught it just as it was to fall to the floor. He viewed the received text placed his phone in his pocket and continued to check his

emails.

The End

Tate was aware he had been shadowed for the better part of a month relating to an alleged pending investigation. He felt a lot of pressure from his political relationship with Raul and he was strained from the relationship in regards to Jeremy Coons. As he dressed for the day Cherry walked into the room, "Is everything ok?" She asked in a concerned voice. "You hardly slept last night." She said. "Yeah just under a lot of stress lately," replied Tate slipping on his favorite red tie.

Cherry wrapped her arms around his waist, "well try not to worry so much the stress will kill you." She said. Tate smiled and continued fiddling with his tie trying to get it to set perfectly in a tight knot. "You're going to need to go out for breakfast babe because I didn't prepare breakfast this morning," said Cherry as she left the house for work. Tate turned on the Television and watched the local news while having his coffee.

The anchorman reported the main news story of the day. "Local politician Anthony Tate has been indicted by the grand jury on corruption charges." The report said.

"Son-of-a bitch," shouted Tate aloud as he watched the report. Tate got on the phone and called his attorney, "Have you heard the news?" Tate Inquired.

"Yeah apparently the got a break in their investigation which gave them the evidence to confidently convict you," said the attorney. "I will make a couple of calls to some folks that owe me a favor and find out the details of what's going on," he said.

"Great," said Tate.

"Come to the office when you're available and let's hash this thing out," said the attorney.

"Yeah," replied Tate as he hung up the phone. Tate knew the consequences if he was indicted which meant forfeiture of his retirement benefits for his family among other issues. Tate called Ray's phone twice and got a busy tone each time, "Damn it Ray." Tate got the keys to his SUV and drove around to clear his head. He wondered where Ray was and why he wasn't answering his cell phone. He decided to drive by Ray's mother's house to see if he had over slept. Tate drove through Ray's neighborhood and did not see the MayBach parked in the yard. He tried Ray's cell number a third time and got the same busy signal tone. "Damn it Ray, where are you." He exclaimed. He decided to check in with his attorney and find out more information on what was going on.

***

Tate arrived at his attorney's office in Coral Gables and hurriedly entered the building for the meeting. "Amp I found out what's happening," said the attorney as Tate entered. "You have been under surveillance by the DEA's office for about two months now and from what I heard they had a hard time digging something up on you," he said. "Your association with that Jeremy Coons kid raised eyebrows with law enforcement," said the attorney. "Jeremy was in the drug game for a long time and got himself arrested on the docks about a month ago for trafficking." Tate paced the floor and then flopped down on a nearby couch in the office. "Jeremy to keep from going to jail decided to become a government informant," he said. "He has been setting people up and the feds has been building cases on a number of individuals," stated the attorney.

"Has Jeremy been indicted?" Ray asked.

"No but your introduction of Jeremy to Commissioner Sancho and his partner sent up another red flag," said the attorney. "Chris Magoya had a private party at the Cabaret and Jeremy supplied all the drugs for the event which was all caught on tape by the feds," the attorney stated. "You didn't listen to the entire news report did you Amp," the attorney commented. "The chief, Commissioner Sancho, and Chris Magoya were indicted as well," he said. "At the party caught on tape are a couple of high ranking officers to include the Chief and Chris Magoya."

Tate sat with his mouth wide open, "I was so shocked by the news report and missed that entire broadcast," said Tate. "Why was Raul indicted," Tate inquired. "Well, Chris decided he wanted to save his rear end by giving Commissioner Sancho up to law enforcement by snitching about their shady business with the City." Tate rubbed his head asked, "Why was I indicted?"

The attorney shifted in his seat and said, "Yesterday the feds picked Ray Sutter up for probation violation for hitting Jeremy in the head with a hammer." Tate looked at the attorney in shock.

"Are you serious?" He questioned.

"Apparently Ray didn't know that Jeremy was a government informant and the feds have the entire incident recorded," said the attorney. "Ray has agreed to bring evidence against you for bribery and whatever other improprieties they plan to hit you with," he said. "Since they can't get you or Commissioner Sancho on narcotics they've turned all their findings over to the state attorney's office."

Tate sighed and reclined back into the couch. Tate with all his good intentions thought he was doing a good deed in employing Ray with work and now Ray will possibly be the main instrument of his ruin.

"You do know if you're convicted you will lose your pension," the attorney stated. "You need to take steps to provide for your family in case of the worst situation," he said. Tate turned before leaving the office. "Did you forget, I did attend law school," Tate replied.

Tate left the office with a heavy heart and he was under pressure to make a crucial decision. As a politician and above all as a man he was responsible for the decisions he made that got him to his point. Mercilessly he strived to provide the best for his community and for the people he cared about. Thwart by detractors the entire time of his political service he sojourned on. Tate drove around the city and pondered his predicament unsure of what to do. He thought maybe he could talk with Ron Wiggins and work with him in presenting his case to the public letting his story be heard. Tate drove to the Miami News building parked and entered the first floor lobby.

He compiled all his documents pertaining to Raul's involvement with the developer regarding the Overtown Development Corporation. All the financial records and payments he had detailed in a black satchel he carried under his arm. He waited in line at the security scan entrance to be scanned in by the armed guards. Behind him two gentlemen were having a conversation concerning the charges against Tate. They were unaware the commissioner was standing less than a foot in front of them.

"Yeah that commissioner Tate is screwed," said the first guy. "He didn't know that Ron Wiggins was planted by Chris Magoya to keep tabs on him about the casino development." Chills ran up Tate's spin when he heard that comment. Things all fell in place now, Ron's mysterious introduction to him and all the information he seemed to effortlessly acquire.

Ron played him the entire time and giving him the documents equated to suicide. As the guard did a body search of the person in front of him Tate snatched his gun out of its holster. Snapped the safety to fire and pulled the trigger.

Thomas Barr Jr.

Thanks for reading; Overlords Karma by Thomas Barr Jr. We hope you enjoyed his first release. Be sure to leave a review and visit our website for more titles from PRINTHOUSE BOOKS Author's.

PRINTHOUSE BOOKS
Read it, Enjoy it, Tell a friend.

VIP INK Publishing Group, Incorporated.
Atlanta, GA.

www.PrintHouseBooks.com

www.ingramcontent.com/pod-product-compliance
Lightning Source LLC
Chambersburg PA
CBHW060346030726
47497CB00003B/612